The Woman Who Forgot Her Agenda

Alexandra Filia

www.loveisagame.net

Edited by Oliver Whiskard
Imprint: Independently published
Cover Painting by the Author

The Woman Who Forgot Her Agenda/ Alexandra Filia. -- 1st ed.
ISBN 978-1-6580481-6-3

DEDICATION

This book is dedicated to my daughters, Katerina and Nina, who are too busy to read my books. Girls, life is a dance, not a journey. Enjoy it! It goes really fast.

CONTENTS

Chapter One

The decision

Each suburban wife struggles with it alone. As she made the beds, shopped for groceries, matched slipcover material, ate peanut butter sandwiches with her children, chauffeured Cub Scouts and Brownies, lay beside her husband at night—she was afraid to ask even of herself the silent question—'Is this all?'

— Betty Friedan, The Feminine Mystique (1963)

Ana Sanderson was furiously looking for her purse. Where had she put it now? During all the dramatic exits in her life, she had always found herself looking for her keys, wallet, coat, whatever it was that was preventing her from making the dramatic exit she wanted. She kept up the stream of complaints to distract her incredulous audience.

"Nobody does anything in this house. I'm nothing more than a maid! I'm sick and tired of looking after everyone else but me." Her husband, Bill, paid no attention. She looked over at her daughters accusingly.

"I always put things away," Linda protested, "and it's Hannah that leaves her laundry on the floor."

"You never ever pick up anything, not even your own plate to put in the dishwasher. The bin is overflowing again. Who tried to squeeze this last yoghurt pot and split the bag at the bottom? Who is going to clean this up?" The conversation made her tired. It's always the same story, the same excuses and promises, but zero action. She admitted defeat. "Where is that damn bag?"

Hannah lifted her coat and unveiled the missing purse. "Here it is mum," she said. "I am sorry."

Ana looked up, assessing her daughter's tone. Was there a tinge of sarcasm? Too fired up to give it a second thought, she reminded herself that nothing ever changes. She grabbed her purse out of Hannah's hand, made sure her keys were rattling at the bottom, and turned on her heel, giving the door a satisfying slam as she walked out.

"I'm done with all of you!" were the final words she left lingering in front of the three pairs of eyes staring back at her. With their mouths slightly open in surprise, her family reminded her of newborn chicks waiting for their next meal.

On the way to her car, she started to feel guilty, but shook the familiar feeling away. This time she would not back down. Something had changed inside her. A switch had been flipped, and things would never be the same again in the Sanderson household. They had awoken a giant!

She fumbled for her car keys, but what she fished out were the other keys to their rental flat. In a flash she remembered that the keys were sitting in the ceramic bowl in the hallway. Could she sneak back inside the house and get them without anyone noticing? Of course not! The house key was tethered to the car key. Deflated, she walked back. Beginning to end, this revolution had lasted seven minutes. Hesitating at the front door, she took a deep breath and rang the doorbell. Hannah let her in. "I forgot my keys," she mumbled. She put her bag down and walked to the kitchen. On her way, she picked up a discarded glass and absentmindedly put it in the dishwasher. Her daughter's voice snapped her out of her daydream.

"That was Linda's glass. I put mine away."

Ana surveyed the living room and counted at least three more glasses on various surfaces. In the distance, she heard the dryer beeping to alert the household that it was the end of the cycle. Nobody but her seemed to be hearing it. Maybe it's like a dog whistle. Only mothers are supposed to hear it. She smelled last night's chicken as its aroma rose out of the overfilled bin.

Her resolve strengthened. This time it would be different. She walked back to the hallway, put the correct keys in her pocket, picked up her bag and walked to the door. As an afterthought, she turned and faced Hannah. "Dinner is in the oven, and there is a salad in the fridge. Don't forget to empty the dryer." With her duties discharged, she headed out.

.

Chapter Two

Freedom

On the way to her little grey Toyota Yaris, Ana started singing. Without anyone there to complain or tell her to stop, she sung louder and pulled away from the curb. Soon she was singing at full blast, and the strength of her voice surprised her. She tried a little scream. It felt hugely satisfying. Not caring if she could be heard from the street, she screamed again, this time much louder and longer. As dramatic as it may sound, she felt like she was expelling a ball of black slime that had been sitting inside her for years.

She felt lighter and even a teensy bit happy. Not the kind of happy she felt after a long sip from a glass of chilled pinot grigio. No, this was a different sort of happy. She looked through the rearview mirror at the deserted road, rolled down the windows and stepped on the gas. She barrelled around the first turn and then the next. She had not driven like this in decades. She used to be a pretty fast driver. Not that anyone in her family knew this. She always did the school run at the speed limit. *Safety first* was an obligation instilled into her from the very first day she became responsible for caring for her valuable cargo, her precious baby daughters. Now she mostly drove alone, but she still drove like her granny. Always slowly, absentmindedly, carefully. She stepped on the gas again.

With sudden fury, she whizzed around the corner while pulling the hand brake. The car fishtailed and then straightened out. She whooped with delight. She still had it! Without letting go of the wheel, she pulled out her iPhone 5 and plugged it in. She should get the latest iPhone. Everyone in the family had the newer models. In fact, she had bought them herself as presents. The injustice hit her, and she winced. And the car, what was she thinking when she bought this piece of shit? It's grey, stubby and reliable. Just like her. When did she become this? She pushed these depressing thoughts away. Things were going to change.

Ana opened Spotify. She had a playlist for times like this. Bon Jovi blared out of the small speakers. *It's my life, and it's now or never. I ain't gonna live forever.* Something inside her stirred. She felt strong, beautiful, powerful. She felt like herself.

Chapter Three

Herself, 1978

Ideally, what should be said to every child, repeatedly, throughout his or her school life is something like this: "You are in the process of being indoctrinated. We have not yet evolved a system of education that is not a system of indoctrination...What you are being taught here is an amalgam of current prejudice and the choices of this particular culture."

— Doris Lessing, The Golden Notebook (1962)

Ana put down her paintbrush and wiped her brow. She stepped back to admire her work. The multi-coloured psychedelic mural covered the entire garage door of their smart end-of-terrace house. Several neighbours were staring aghast, and Mrs Trent, who lives across the street and has the best view of her artwork, seemed to be profoundly disturbed by the new addition to her view. Unruffled, Ana collected her art supplies and walked around to the back garden to rinse her brushes. In the corner of her eye she saw her mum's slippers approaching. Eventually, their eyes met. She defiantly held her gaze, fully expecting a verbal lashing, but she was surprised to see the first hints of a smile on her mother's face.

"I think Mrs Trent may have a stroke she is so red. As for your dad, well you know what he's like. I think you will need to paint over your artwork, sweetheart, but let's take some pictures first. I will tell your dad that I asked you to paint the garage door and your creative flair took over, ok?"

Ana nodded, satisfied. She had made her point and confirmed to the neighbourhood once again that she was a rebel. Nobody messes with her. Nobody.

At fifteen, Ana was a bit of a terror. Her mother, Debby, had given up trying to control her and was satisfied just knowing that Ana wasn't failing her courses. As for everything else, she hoped that she would grow out of it. Ana had a kind heart under her rebellious exterior, and the bond between mother and daughter was healthy. Despite all her bravado, Ana wanted to be liked, especially by her mum. After the two of them shared a pizza, she quietly went back to work and painted over her art. Mrs Trent looked smug, so Ana mumbled loud enough for Mrs Trent to hear, "the colours were all wrong. I will try something brighter next time."

Ana was never sure who she was rebelling against, and she often felt that the whole world was against her. All you needed to do was tell her that she couldn't do something, and she would put all her energy into that particular thing until she succeeded. This was especially true for things that were unladylike, things that only boys did. She had this fire inside her, striving to prove to the world that she was good.

She was better than the boys who had the freedom to go out and try things.

Ana grew up in North London, the eldest of Debby and Nick's two daughters. Her younger sister Tracy did not resemble her in any way. She was blonde, short and skinny, and loved to play with dolls. She hosted elaborate tea parties with them, with real miniature muffins and cupcakes baked in the oven. Ana, who had never hosted a tea party herself, often walked in on her sister's events to lecture the girls about women's independence. But this was mainly an excuse to sample the delicately decorated tea cakes.

Debby and Nick encouraged both of their daughters to try new things and be independent and self-sufficient. While Tracy was compliant and very much a mummy's girl, Ana took every opportunity to test her parent's patience. Raising Ana was no easy task, but her parents did the best they could to keep their wild daughter in check while not clipping her wings. When at age five she refused to put on her pink tutu and go to ballet class because there were no boys there, her decision was respected, and they signed her up for swimming lessons instead.

But her parents weren't always consistent with their views. They wanted their girls to be independent, but at the same time they believed that a good marriage and children should be the ultimate goal of every woman. When Ana developed "swimming shoulders" after a couple of years in the pool, her mum abruptly ended her swimming career for fear that her unladylike physique would drive potential husbands away.

"I don't care about husbands," Ana wailed. But this was no use. Her days in the pool were over.

Then she was signed up for tennis at the local club, which was also a social gathering place for kids of the upper crust.

"A great place for Ana to meet new friends, and in time a suitable boyfriend," she overheard her mum saying to her dad.

Ana didn't think that she would ever have a boyfriend. She didn't like boys very much. But then again, she didn't like girls either. Any girl that refused to try this or that because she was "a girl" immediately went on Ana's bad list, and most girls she met ended up on that list sooner or later. As she got older, the list started to include any girl who couldn't do something because it was that time of the month. Perhaps she was just fortunate to never experience any discomfort during her periods, but she knew that girls used it as an excuse to avoid PE.

"These girls make us all look bad," she complained to her long-suffering mum who had heard it all before and was half listening while loading the dishwasher.

"Yes, I see what you mean," she mumbled. "You don't do that, do you?"

Ana was used to her mum half-listening and not really paying attention to her ramblings. She was always so busy taking care of everyone and everything.

Ana loaded up her plate with the leftover pizza and plopped herself on the sofa in front of the TV. "I'll never get married," she declared. "None of these jokers deserve me."

Chapter Four

Who is this woman?

Still giddy from her drive, Ana stormed into the house. She marched through the kitchen and faced her family, all sitting in a row in front of the TV.

"I'm back," she declared.

Nobody looked up. She couldn't help but notice the trail of plates, bags, coats and glasses that decorated every surface, as well as a good part of the floor and hallway. But this new Ana refused to pick up anything. Without a word, she marched upstairs and locked the bedroom door behind her. What she wanted to do next required no witnesses.

Ana dove into the wardrobe and searched for her scales, feeling around the furthest corners. She eventually fished them out, gave them a quick wipe, and then without hesitation stripped and stepped on. Wow! No wonder her knees hurt! 78 kilos! She must have been the fattest she had ever been. Ana turned to the mirror. A creased face, with tired eyes and a deep scowl stared back at her. She had to do her roots. She needed a hairdresser urgently. She remembered trying to squeeze in an appointment not that long ago, but it proved impossible to coordinate her duties with the hairdresser's busy schedule. In an act of defiance, she picked up the phone and booked the first available appointment. *Hair, tick!* If only the rest were as easy. The magnitude of the task ahead threatened to overwhelm her into inaction.

She marched into her daughter's bedroom and picked up a notebook. She carefully tore off the first few pages with Hannah's sparse notes and left them on her desk chair. She knew her daughter well. She might as well have thrown them in the bin for all the revision that Hannah had done or would ever do. She rummaged in the desk drawer for a pen that wasn't pink, glittery pink, or scented purple. Then, thinking better of it, she grabbed the glittery pink one and retreated to her secure haven. Shutting and locking the door behind her, she tried to lay on the carpet face down like she used to. The manoeuvre proved very uncomfortable, and she briefly wondered why, before sitting on the edge of the bed instead. She opened the notebook and let the pen hover above the page for a minute before writing her first objective:

1. Lose 20 kilos

Then she stalled. What else? To her surprise, nothing else came to her. Remembering her little grey Toyota, she added:

2. Get a new car

Her husband Bill always got the new car, the bigger and better car. Even though he couldn't drive for shit, his privilege was uncontested. He was the man, and he drove us in his nice car, which she wasn't even allowed to drive. Her car was used for ferrying the kids, shopping and other mundane chores that were beneath him. Bill earned the money in the family and took care of the mortgage, so he deserved the nice car. Her blood began to boil like never before. When they met, at work, she had the MBA, the better job and the bigger salary. With the second baby arriving quickly on the heels of the first, she had to reluctantly resign. The agreement was that she would return to work when the second baby was old enough to go to Reception, but somehow it never happened. Life got in the way, and Bill insisted that they couldn't afford the daycare for two kids, not to mention the cooking, cleaning, shopping, and laundry. The possibility of him doing the housework and her going back to work was never discussed.

He even tried to convince her that she got the better deal. As she sat folding the laundry, knee-deep in toddler toys, he declared that he wished he could take time off work to be with the kids. Work was just too stressful.

"Why don't you?" she replied.

"Oh, you know what happens when men become househusbands. The sex is over."

Ana pondered the consequences of the sex being over, and she silently wished that Bill was a house husband. That, of course, was many moons ago when they still had sex. The sex had ended as her duties multiplied and neither party showed any interest in resuming relations. She wondered at times whether he was getting some on the side, but the prospect didn't worry her at all. Her attitude on the matter was that as long as she didn't know about it, she didn't care what he did.

She put pen to paper and wrote:

3. Get back to work

She had to get back to work before she could get a new car. She mentally added up the years since her second maternity leave. Sixteen years! An eternity when it comes to modern finance. Her degree might as well have been on the migratory habits of the arctic tern. She cast her mind back to the part-time jobs and voluntary work she had done in the last decade and pondered whether she could spin any of this to build her CV and fill the employment gaps since Linda was born. No, she decided. Certainly not for the kind of job she wanted to do.

Discouraged, she closed the notebook and hid it in a drawer next to her side of the bed. She couldn't be bothered to squeeze into her clothes again, so she wrapped herself in the faded housecoat hanging behind the door to the en suite. Did she really go out and buy this? It's awful. The colour, the shape, everything. She took it off, rolled it into a ball and threw it in the wastepaper bin. Rummaging through her wardrobe, she pulled out a pair of leggings and a comfortable jumper. They fit, but barely.

"A small triumph!" she declared to nobody. Her spirits lifted a little bit. She reopened the notebook and made one last entry with Hannah's pink glittery pen:

4. Clear my wardrobe

She hesitated over the discarded housecoat. The decision had to stick. She would not be seen looking like a middle-aged woman, beaten up by life. With a flourish, almost like a ceremony, she picked up her scissors and cut up the offending housecoat, before throwing the pieces back in the bin. She then turned around and went downstairs to join her unsuspecting family.

Chapter Five

Thomas, 1984

"Oh mum he is a dream, and he totally gets me."

Ana was in love. She fell in love just as her family was starting to believe that she would never marry. She had shown zero interest in boys. While her friends dated and brought boyfriends home for study dates, Ana stuck to the few girls that had earned her respect. They were fearless, wild girls, who acted more like boys. Girls with grand plans and a mind of their own. Ana's mum was of two minds about letting them near her daughter.

On the one hand, these girls recognised that the route to the independence they craved involved a lot of hard work. They studied and quizzed each other endlessly, and their grades reflected their singlemindedness. But on the other hand, they were easy to anger over the smallest things, and their temper flared uncontrollably when anyone pointed out that they couldn't do this or that because they were girls.

"Who is going to want to have a relationship with a girl like that?" wondered Ana's mum. "They will end up on the shelf without a husband or a family."

Ana just laughed. "Don't worry mum, and we're not lesbians. We just want a lot more out of life than a husband and a family."

Just as her mum was losing all hope, Ana met Thomas and fell for him hard. Suddenly the house started to smell of nail polish and hairspray, and new beauty products sprang up in the bathroom. Ana's voice had a new tone when she was on the phone. A sweet womanly tone that her mum didn't think her daughter was capable of producing. At eighteen, Ana was quite a beauty, and it didn't take long for Thomas to have feelings for her in return. Within a few months they were inseparable and started planning their life together. They would be at the same university. Life was roses.

Then they rented a flat together to house their blossoming love affair. Soon, they were surrounded by mountains of dirty plates, laundry and takeaway pizza boxes. Neither of them thought it was their job to clean up, cook or scrub the toilet. Thomas, at first lovingly and sweetly, and then insistently, spoke to Ana about bringing some order to the chaos around them. "Why don't you pick up your stuff baby? We can't live like this, on takeaways. Why don't you cook something nice?"

Ana was unsure why she was expected to clean and cook. What about him? Thomas didn't seem to be doing anything of practical value either. All he did was mouth instructions, waiting for her to become a carbon copy of his mother.

Thomas' mother made a visit, spurred by her son's cries for mothering and attention. She despaired at Ana's inability to keep house and feed her son. She gently tried to instruct her on the ways of a woman. Ana's reaction was less than respectful, leaving her shocked and worried about what her son had gotten himself into. She spent an entire day cooking, cleaning, ironing and stocking the fridge and cupboards with Thomas's favourite foods, hoping that Ana would pick up the baton and follow her example when she cooled down, which of course, she didn't.

What she did instead was draw up a chart of chores and rotas, which she placed on the kitchen door. When Thomas came home from his lectures, he spent a few minutes looking at the chart and then at Ana. His posture changed and something stirred behind the eyes.

"Ana, this isn't working out. You want to turn me into a wimp. Men don't do these jobs, these are all women's jobs. I expected more from you. I work hard on my degree so that I can get a good job and we can have a family, and you're doing nothing to help."

Ana turned several shades of purple as she tried to digest the unfairness of what she had just heard. Then she let it rip.

"You are an inconsequential chauvinist pig! What makes you think I have to take care of you while I'm doing *my* degree? Do you think that I'll just depend on a guy for my whole life and not have a job and my own money?" She gathered her things and piled them in her suitcase. She stopped and looked up at him. "Actually, why should I move out? You go. Pack your shit and get out."

Which he did. So ended Ana's first intimate relationship with the opposite sex.

Chapter Six

And here is where it all begins

No woman gets an orgasm from shining the kitchen floor.

— Betty Friedan

Ana had a bad night. She twisted and turned in the dark, trying not to wake up Bill. As dawn broke, she tiptoed out of the bedroom, clutching her notebook, her resolve even stronger than the night before. At the kitchen door, she stopped. All the dishes from the night before were still on the table, leftovers and all. The milk sat on the counter, forgotten by the last person who made tea the night before. She walked past the mess, emptied the spoiled milk into the sink, and made herself a strong black coffee. Coffee in one hand and the notebook and glittery pink pen in the other, she curled up on the sofa to contemplate her next move.

She looked at her number one goal, which was to lose weight. She knew that a goal had to be measurable, achievable, and have a date. She wrote underneath: "Lose 20 kilos in 5 months." She decided not to tell anyone. Not that they would notice, they were so self-absorbed. She turned to a fresh page and wrote a list of tasks.

Shop for healthy items
Clear the cupboards of temptations
Weigh in once a week
Join Weight Watchers
Join the gym

She worked through the list methodically, starting with the cupboards. Without stopping to think, she chucked out the chocolates, crisps, biscuits, and sugary drinks and cereals. Then she moved on to the fridge like a woman possessed. Cheese, ice cream, half a cake, and a pot of double cream went into the bin. Satisfied, she logged on to her online Tesco account and loaded the weekly shop with fruit, veg, grains, herbal teas and a few healthy ready meals for emergencies. After a brief pause, she cancelled the case of white wine and replaced it with a single bottle. She clicked the checkout button and took another sip from her rapidly cooling coffee.

She had read about the power of flow, and she knew that it must feel the way she felt this morning. Everything was effortless. By the time Bill staggered into the kitchen, rubbing his eyes, she had joined Weight Watchers and researched the local gyms.

"Can I have a coffee and an omelette please?" Bill asked, expecting nothing less than warm compliance. Having turned around, he turned back to realise that she was gone. He sat down, expecting her to reappear shortly, perhaps carrying the ironing board to press his shirt. He noticed that she hadn't brought in the paper yet, so he reluctantly went to the front door to fetch it. Unwilling to wait any longer, he brewed a cup of coffee and sat down, waiting for his wife to return and get busy making his omelette. He had to make some space, because last night's dishes were somehow still all over the table. He returned to his paper, waiting to be served. A quarter of an hour passed, and he realised that Ana was not going to return in time to make his breakfast. Unhappy, he shuffled upstairs looking for her. He found her in his office, busily writing on her laptop.

"What are you doing?" he said. "It's late, and now I have to go to work without breakfast. And the kitchen is a mess."

"I hope you cleaned it then," Ana said, without looking away from the screen.

Not used to his wife being belligerent, Bill didn't push the matter further. He dressed quickly and left the house, hoping that whatever this was would pass by the time he got home for dinner. He put it down to it being her time of the month, as he walked to the tube station.

An hour later, Hannah and Linda walked into the kitchen. "Yack!" they exclaimed in unison.

"This is gross! Mum, mum, mum! Mum?"

They sat down facing each other and as far away from the dirty dishes as possible. Then they pulled out their iPhones, and one by one they saw the time.

"Mum, mum." They ran upstairs looking for Ana. The solver of all problems was serenely sitting in front of her laptop, typing furiously.

"Mum, why did you not wake us up? We missed the bus, and now we're going to be late for school!"

She looked up. "Then you better hurry. Give your mother a kiss and get going quickly."

They looked at their mum with gaping mouths. No sound came out, and not knowing what else to do, they turned around and hurried to get ready. They got into their uniform in record time and left for school, having skipped breakfast, not brushed their teeth, and forgetting half their schoolbooks. Ana smiled to herself. This is what she called a good start.

Chapter Seven

A very independent and driven young lady

Ana thought long and hard about what had happened with Thomas. She was unsure how it had all gone so wrong. When Thomas broke up with her, she spent days crying in the empty apartment. She did all the things she had refused to do when Thomas was around, and the apartment looked the tidiest it had ever looked, but she couldn't accept that these small practicalities were the reason for the breakup. Her friends and her mum suggested that she call him to try to patch things up.

"The whole thing happened for a ridiculous reason," said her best friend Meghan. "He is probably regretting it already. All you have to do is give him a call and invite him over. I'm sure he's just looking for an opening to get back together. Promise him that you will be neater and cook once in a while and I am sure things will work themselves out."

Ana was way too proud to do any of this. Instead, she cried, drank wine and wrote feminist diatribes in her diary until the raw pain passed. Eventually she was ready to have a chat with mum.

Ana's mum came to visit on a weekend to soothe her daughter's pain and ruffled feathers. She tried to explain what was expected of a woman, but Ana found the whole thing to be too outlandish to even consider.

"Mum, Thomas is a modern man, there is absolutely no way that he expected me to take care of everything. He is not a baby and we're both going to university full time."

Her mum took a deep breath and tried again to domesticate her daughter. "Ana, sweetheart, men never really grow up. It's up to us women to keep the household going. We see what needs to be done. They don't even notice until they run out of underwear, or there's no food on the table or beer in the fridge."

Ana scoffed at her mum's advice. "You are so far behind the times mum. Thomas couldn't possibly have expected me to cook and clean after him. How would I have found the time to do everything? Also, I wouldn't even know where to start. It's not like I know how to cook, or even use a vacuum."

Her mum stopped in her tracks. She had never asked Ana to do anything when she lived at home. Occasionally, they baked cakes together, but it wasn't Ana's favourite thing to do. She should have done a better job with Ana. She hesitated. Could she have done a better job? She wasn't an easy or compliant child. She thought she knew everything, and the private girls' school she attended never offered a home economics class, far from it. Instead, they taught the girls to seek equality at home and the workplace, and Ana had taken all these lectures to heart. If she got any hint that she was being discriminated against in any way she would go into a rage and produce a tirade of examples of female oppression. They didn't prepare these girls for the real world, that's for sure. To her daughter, she simply said, "Darling, you have a lot to learn. The world doesn't work the way they taught you at school. If you want to get your way, you will need to learn to manoeuvre yourself differently, like a woman. Men don't like tigers in their home, only in their bed."

Ana was adamant. "Mum, you know nothing!" She walked away, but inside her a seed was beginning to take hold.

Chapter Eight

Pushy woman, ambitious man

Town Bank Holdings was Ana's first real job, and she had certainly earned her spot in the September training class. She got an offer after five interviews, and several tests and assessments. It was a real job in a respected bank, and she was over the moon. She phoned all her friends to let them know and was warmly, if not enviously, congratulated by everyone. Her mum wanted to know about their maternity policy, and Ana couldn't help but marvel at the absurdity of the question.

"Mum! I'm twenty-two years old and my last boyfriend left over a year ago. Maternity is the state I am least likely to find myself in right now."

Ana's start date was a few weeks away, and in her offer was a list of items she would need to have before she could work at the branch.

"Black or dark blue suit, button-up white shirt, sensible black pumps with a small heel, women's floppy bow tie (what the hell is that?), flesh-coloured hose and small earrings in silver or gold." She recited this list to Meghan and they both burst out laughing.

"It reads like an undertaker's wardrobe. Do they expect modern women to dress like that?"

Ana complained, "I don't have a single one of these things. We need to go shopping."

The required uniform made Ana look like a crow, but she thought it was a small price to pay to climb the corporate ladder.

The first few months at the bank were a whirlwind of activity. Ana worked hard and did her best to stand out for all the right reasons, but somehow she felt side-lined and overlooked. Unperturbed, she kept her head down and did what she was told. Not once did she consider that her rise would be anything less than meteoric. She was well educated, smart, hardworking, well-spoken and a real go-getter.

They were introduced to the banks internal evaluation system, called STARS. It measured each person's sales by bank product and by customer, and then assigned a number to each account executive. Every month the STARS ranking was published internally, so everyone could see where they stood compared to their peers. The top person was given a congratulatory note by the regional vice president and local president, and their name got a special mention in the employee newsletter.

Ana loved the STARS system. It was an objective, black and white way to show everyone what she could achieve, and achieve she did. During her six months at the bank, she climbed to the top, and then stayed there month after month, each time widening the gap between her numbers and Steve's, who was the next account executive on the list and a football buddy of the regional vice president. She got along with Steve, a stocky, potbellied man in his mid-twenties. She even went to his engagement party and met his fiancé and family. They had a drink together every Friday to celebrate the week's successes, and Steve seemed to be in awe of her and her meteoric rise in the STARS ranking. He asked for advice and tips, which she was delighted to share.

As the months passed, she waited for her congratulatory note to appear. She had been at the top for three months in a row, totally unacknowledged. Their manager would walk by their desks and pat Steve on the back, but he never even came near her or offered any words of encouragement. Then, on the fourth month, the bank's newsletter landed on her desk. On the front page, she saw Steve's picture.

Steve Brenner smashes it. STARS superhero does it again!

Ana scanned the article. Halfway down she found her name.

Ana Sanderson from the Pittsford branch comes first in the
STARS ranking.

Ana snatched the newsletter with both hands and marched towards her manager Brian's office. She marched in that *Ana* way, resolutely, jutting her jaw so far forward that it always entered first through a doorway. She entered and placed her hands on his desk.

"For four months I have been top of the STARS list, and I haven't received any acknowledgement from anyone. In the newsletter, there is a picture of Steve who is second on the list, and look at this headline." She pointed at the newsletter. "It's very unfair," she said.

Brian was not impressed. He barely tolerated women in his team, having worked almost exclusively with men for his whole career, first as a football coach and then at Town Bank. To have this woman screeching at him in his office and touching his desk was more than he could bear.

"Ms Sanderson, your behaviour is unprofessional and threatening. It is simply unacceptable. I have to ask you to leave my office immediately, and I feel obligated to report your outburst to Human Resources. If you have a complaint to discuss, you will have to set up a meeting. For your information, Steve has been a consistent performer for two years now, and this is why I chose him to be featured in the newsletter."

"You chose him because he's a man and he's your football buddy," she raged.

"You are pushy and abrasive," he said. "In this bank we like ambitious people, but your sales style is not what we're after in a model employee."

For a moment, Ana just stood there, taking in the injustice of what just happened. When she looked up and saw Brian's tight lips and contorted face, she realised that she had gone too far, and that the best strategy would be to retreat.

"I'm sorry for my outburst," she mumbled. "I will set up a meeting later in the week to discuss this matter." She tried to moderate her voice, but what came out sounded vaguely threatening. Ana returned to her desk. She had a load of calls to make and deals to close, but her heart wasn't in it. It turns out that this didn't matter anyway. Before the end of the day, she was put on probation, and within a month she had lost her job at the bank.

In the months that followed, she questioned whether Brian was right. When she got a new job, she moderated her behaviour to suit what was expected of a female employee.

Chapter Nine

A friend in need

Ana couldn't concentrate. Editing her CV was giving her a headache. It had been years since she had to do anything more complicated than organise a play date or follow a recipe. For starters, it was on a floppy disk, which meant that she had to go into the attic and dig out the old Dell computer and then figure out how to connect it to the internet. Assuming that it even worked. When her best friend Meghan visited, she found Ana sitting on the top step of the stairs, going through a box of old photos, letters, and the odd dried-out flower.

Meghan was wearing baggy jeans and an old checked shirt under a fraying green cardigan. It was a *busy mummy* outfit much like her. Meghan always went for comfort over style, but today this made Ana strangely uncomfortable. Is this how she, too, dresses? She looked down at her own baggy corduroys, topped by a jumper that Hannah had discarded. Meghan dropped her bag on the floor and plopped herself on the step next to Ana.

"Hi Ana, ready to go?"

"Go? Go where?" Then Ana remembered. "Ah, the cake sale. Shit, I forgot all about it. Do we have to go? I've started a diet and I'm also in the middle of updating my CV."

"Your CV? Is it in that box? Why are you updating your CV?"

"I got side-tracked. I'm looking for a computer that reads floppy disks and there's one in the attic. My CV is on this disk." Ana waved the floppy disk in Meghan's general direction.

Meghan let out a laugh. "You can't be serious. This thing is ancient. The data on it is probably corrupt. If you want to update your CV, you may as well start from scratch. It will be quicker. Want help?"

"You are a life saver. Yes, I can use all the help I can get. Let me grab some paper". Ana went down the stairs and disappeared into the kitchen where she had left her notebook.

Meghan had been Ana's friend since high school. Together they backpacked around Europe, double-dated and babysat each other's kids. They got married within months of each other and for the past thirty years they've been inseparable. Meghan married her college sweetheart and gave up her mediocre career as a sales assistant to a broker right away. Her main ambition of getting married fulfilled, she proceeded to have a brood of babies and spent her days planning her next step on the property ladder.

Ana noticed that Meghan had moved after the birth of each of her four children, and every two years after the last one had gone to nursery. The years had been kind to Meghan. Unlike Ana, she still had the body of her youth, probably the result of regular yoga classes and running after four children. But, like Ana, her hair had not seen a hairdresser in years and her home hair dye was a few shades off her natural colour. Neither woman spent much on herself. They didn't see the point. Their wrinkles were life badges, and the extra money in the family budget was better spent on the children.

Ana walked into the living room and sat down next to her friend, opening the notebook to a fresh page. She looked at her friend quizzically. Meghan seemed content.

"Tell me Meghan, do you ever wonder whether we wasted our lives? We got terrific degrees and we had career plans. What happened? Is this all there is? Is it too late to start something new?"

Meghan smiled. "So this is what got into you? Midlife crisis, eh? Don't worry. It passes. Sign up for a painting course or something and you will feel better. Do you want to go to a yoga retreat? We can go together and take some time off from the kids. What do you think?"

Ana looked up at her friend. "Midlife crisis? Maybe. But I'm being serious. I want to change my life. I have become invisible, a servant. I don't matter."

"Don't be ridiculous, of course you matter. You matter to your kids, Bill, me and many others I'm sure. What would they do without you?"

"They would get a maid, that's what they would do!" Ana blurted, without any trace of humour. Next, Ana meant to say that she wanted to earn her own money, but to her own surprise she said, "I want a new car and I want to go on a road trip, alone."

Meghan had no doubt that Ana was capable of finding the money to buy a car and take off on her own. She had seen Ana do remarkable things with little thought or planning and she knew that her friend was determined and fearless. Something stirred inside her and she realised that she was envious of Ana's newfound determination and vitality. If Ana followed her dreams, she would feel old and left behind. She pushed that thought away, determined to feel proud for her friend and not clip her wings in any way.

"Okay, she said, let's look at that CV."

Heads huddled together, the two friends spent the whole morning and a good part of the afternoon putting together Ana's CV. They checked dates, degrees, workshops, references, and carefully typed it all up using a template suggested by the computer. When the new CV rolled out of the printer, they both looked at it with wonder. It was Ana's ticket to freedom and they both felt it.

With the first step of her new agenda completed, Ana was going to pour them both a celebratory glass of chardonnay. But then she remembered her diet and offered her friend a diet soda instead.

"So, what's your next move?" Meghan inquired, impressed by her friend's resolve.

"I've signed up for evening CPD courses to catch up with the professional world. I'm rusty, but I have the basic knowledge, so it shouldn't take long. It will be harder to convince employers to take me on. Most of the companies on my CV don't even exist anymore." Ana sipped at her drink, considering her options. "My last job was senior manager, but to start I will apply for admin jobs through a temp agency. I'm a fast typist and I can get a job within a week, I am quite sure. I want to start earning my own money as soon as possible. Come upstairs, I want your opinion on something."

Ana ran upstairs two steps at a time and Meghan trailed behind her marvelling at her energy. The king-sized bed was covered with what seemed to be the entire contents of Ana's wardrobe. "I'm doing a clear-out," Ana explained. "But for now, I need to decide on an interview outfit."

They spent the rest of the afternoon going through Ana's clothes, trying to find something suitable. Seeing her wardrobe through the eyes of an employer, Ana quickly realised that she had nothing to work with. Her clothes reflected how she saw her life. Old, tired, and ready to be thrown away. This wouldn't do. Everything would have to go in the bin. In the fading light, and with Meghan's help, she filled several bin bags with the worst offenders. She wasn't even sure that the homeless would want it. She sighed and sat on the floor in her underwear, exhausted. Meghan pulled a black skirt from the back of the closet and Ana recognised it as the one she had bought for Bill's uncle's funeral a couple of years back.

"Does this fit you?" Meghan asked, waiving the skirt in her direction. Ana tried it on and it fit! There was also a shirt to go with it. She was now ready to join the world of the newly employed.

Together they carried the bin bags to the curb and Ana hugged her friend. "Thank you so much for today. It was epic what we did. It would have taken me a week without you."

Meghan laughed. "You go get them. Do it for all of us. Go ahead, start the revolution of the trodden down mummy!" With that she got in her car and drove off to cook dinner for her family. That evening, in Ana's house, they ate the first of many takeaway pizza meals. Ana didn't touch the pizza which she knew was five hundred calories a slice. She slowly munched through a plate of salad and hard-boiled eggs, while scanning through the job ads on her computer. Change was in the air, and it made her feel powerful.

Chapter Ten

Berkeley, San Francisco Bay

Warm Californian wind blew Ana's hair as she stepped off the plane in San Francisco. The last few months had been a whirlwind of unexpected activity. The debacle at Town Bank made Ana re-evaluate her future and, in what seemed like a spur of the moment decision, she applied for an MBA. More degrees, more choices. She wanted to make sure that what happened at the bank never happened to her again.

UC Berkeley was not an easy choice to make, if for no other reason than she couldn't afford it, but the reputation of the school as a hotbed of activism made up her mind. She wanted an environment where she could express herself and be recognised for her effort and ability. America promised to be all of these things. UC Berkeley was near the recently booming Silicon Valley, where she hoped to get an internship or even a full-time job after graduation. When her offer letter landed on her front door, Ana was overjoyed. She knew that there was no way she could afford the fees on her own, but she was determined to go, come hell or high water. Her dad, of course, declined the opportunity to mortgage the family home on his daughter's whim and emigrate to the US. Undeterred, Ana took on two jobs and saved every penny. Admiring Ana's determination and hard work, he finally relented, as Ana knew he would, and came up with half the money before her offer letter expired.

Ana relied heavily on being able to work in San Francisco and her visa allowed her to work part-time during term time and full-time between terms. With her experience at Town Bank, she felt confident that she would find something to tide her over.

She took a deep breath and drank in the view from campus. The bay stretched below her, and she truly felt on top of the world. Standing at that spot, right then, was all her doing. She thought about it, planned it, and made it happen. Her confidence was soaring, much more than usual. In the space of eight months, she was accepted into one of the best MBA programs in the world, worked two jobs to earn a good chunk of the money, got her visa sorted, and now, here she was in San Francisco ready to start her classes with eager anticipation.

Berkeley didn't offer her accommodation at the campus, but she preferred it that way. The university forums were full of students looking for roommates, and she preferred to bunk with people she had a chance of meeting in advance, not to mention having her own room. It was through these forums that she met Julie.

Julie was born in England, but her parents moved to Los Angeles when she was fourteen. She had retained a faint British accent, which sounded extra cute coming from this otherwise typical LA girl. There was something about Julie that attracted Ana right away. Perhaps it was the accent that reminded her of home, or maybe it was the way that Julie opened up—in a very un-English way—during their very first meeting. She was not exactly pretty. She had thin, mousy hair and a less than perfect figure. But she was so confident in her own skin that Ana's first impressions changed as soon as Julie started speaking. She had an aura about her that you couldn't ignore. Julie's hands moved as she started describing the apartment. In fact, her whole body moved with excitement at the possibility of Ana moving in. She described what would be Ana's room, the large kitchen, and the small bathroom that three girls would need to share. But what clinched the deal was the very reasonable amount that she had to pay for rent. Ana moved in that afternoon, happy to escape the dingy hostel she had previously been living in.

With her living arrangements sorted, Ana directed her energy into finding a job. This proved more of a challenge because of the restricted hours that she was allowed to work. She was offered waitress and bar-attendant jobs, but she knew that they wouldn't pay enough to support her through two years of graduate school. Just as she was losing heart, she came upon an unassuming advert looking for a receptionist and admin assistant between the hours of six and nine in the evening, weekends included. The pay seemed ludicrous for the number of hours, so with a healthy dose of suspicion she emailed her CV and cover letter.

Before the end of the week she got invited to an interview. The address was near the campus in a wealthy part of town. Wearing her smartest outfit from her days at the bank, she arrived at the interview a few minutes early and was buzzed in at the professional-looking reception. Other than the woman interviewing her, the place was deserted.

Ana explained her situation, as well as how desperate she was to get the job. She was surprised by some of the questions but answered everything truthfully. No, she was not religious and yes, she believed that morality was sometimes subjective, and she had a very open mind. It was only after she was offered the job and accepted it that she fully understood why the woman asked her questions that at the time seemed irrelevant. For her new job she was an assistant to a madam who ran an escort service specialising in IT nerds who wanted to meet college girls. Ana didn't mind at all. The pay was great, the hours suited her, and as long as nobody asked her to have sex for money, she was completely fine with everything else. Escort services in California were perfectly legal as long as there was no sex for money involved. Ana wasn't sure this was strictly observed by the girls, but what she didn't know couldn't hurt her.

Chantelle, her new boss, handed her a training manual so that she could familiarise herself with the business. That evening, Ana read parts of it to Julie as they sat on their battered sofa sipping their ginger beers.

"Clients who book escorts in Silicon Valley may or may not be involved in the technology sector, but they are a youngish (twenties to thirties) demographic, smart, and looking for an affable and intelligent companion to take their mind off work. Work hours are long at Silicon Valley and social life can be compromised whereby the client finds it impossible to date women outside of work. A high-class escort agency that operates internationally or locally may be the first port of call for Silicon Valley clients who are looking for a beautiful and sophisticated model to help them unwind. Our agency, Sophisticated Encounters, will suggest things to do with your client, places you can go, and how to enjoy each other's company."

What a job it proved to be. She learned a wealth of information from the girls who crowded the white leather sofa across from her desk. In their impossible high heels and impeccable makeup, they gave her advice about everything from makeup to shopping to catching a man. Occasionally, their advice became more esoteric and often quite racy, and Ana lapped it all up. She was not just learning business here at Berkeley, she was learning how to be a woman that could drive men crazy. Other than the fringe educational benefits, her job was quite mundane and well within her abilities. She updated the website with new girls, answered the phone, and organised taxis to take the girls quickly and safely to their dates. Clients would occasionally take the ladies to the opera or on a cruise around the bay. Every now and again she would recognise girls from the university, but she never mentioned anything to them or anyone else. Discretion was of paramount importance. Chantelle stressed that Ana's lips should be sealed when it came to her job, but Ana made an exception for Julie, who was sworn to secrecy. She entertained Julie regularly with anecdotes from work, but she was very careful to never mention any specific girls. One can never be too careful.

Ana really enjoyed her days at Berkeley, and her grades reflected it. With her job and her friends, she felt *edgy and cool*. With her eye on a Wall Street job she got a subscription to the Wall Street Journal and kept every issue until the growing pile reached the height of the sofa.

"When are you going to get rid of this?" Julie kept complaining, as she vacuumed around the shrine to Wall Street. "It's all out of date anyway. These are dailies you know."

"I promise, I will go through them this weekend," Ana said. But there was no follow through. Julie got rid of the papers herself, by slow degrees, starting at the bottom of the pile. Ana noticed, but she never confronted Julie about it.

When the Wall Street giants came to Berkeley to pick the best and brightest students for a round of interviews, Ana was among the chosen few. In what became the stuff of legend in later years, Ana clinched a job with one of the top firms in Wall street, Silverman Brothers, by pulling a risky stunt. On her final round of interviews, she was asked what sound an ashtray makes when it falls to the ground. Without hesitation, she picked up the heavy crystal ashtray on the desk in front of her and let it drop to the ground where it smashed into a million pieces. Having called his bluff, she looked at the interviewer, a chain-smoking veteran trader, straight in the eye, and smiled. "That's the best way that I know to accurately describe the sound."

He nodded, stood up, and ended the interview. Ana instantly regretted her impulsiveness and left the room, positive that she had ruined her chances.

When the offer letter landed on her doorstep a week later, including an invoice of a hundred dollars for the crystal ashtray, she knew that she had found the perfect job.

The last six months at Berkeley passed in a flash. She almost cried when she said goodbye to Chantelle. In her two years at Sophisticated Encounters, she had helped grow the business by thirty percent by convincing Chantelle to incorporate a small but very profitable male escort service.

Luckily, she didn't have to say goodbye to Julie, who had also got a job in Wall Street working as a trader for a Canadian bank, despite having never read a single issue of the Wall Street Journal. With a bit of trepidation, they agreed to drive across country to save some money and also make an adventure out of their move. Julie had an old Chevy Blazer that was so big it had enough room for the two of them to sleep in the back, along with their belongings. Both families tried to dissuade them, fearing everything from flat tyres to roving rapists, but nothing would change the girls' minds. They were chasing their dreams with the courage of the young and the boldness of the undefeated.

Chapter Eleven

Bill loses his patience

On the third night that he was served leftover pizza, Bill revolted. Without looking away from his iPad he started grunting and showing his displeasure as he pushed the plate away. Ana, who was in the middle of composing a cover letter to a recruiter, responded with a grunt of her own.

"Ana, we can't eat pizza three rays in a row," he complained. "You're at home all day. Can't you cook a proper meal for the family. The girls shot a look towards their mother, but decided not to participate. Ana looked up from her computer and, without a word, picked up Bill's plate, emptied the pizza into the bin, put the plate in the sink and then sat down again in front of her laptop.

Bill understood when he was being challenged and did not like it one bit. "Ana, what's the matter? And how long are you going to keep feeding us this pizza?"

"I have been busy. I am looking for a job," Ana responded, without looking up from her screen.

"A job, a *job*? Why are you looking for a job? You haven't worked in years. Your job is your family and you're neglecting it. This morning there were no ironed shirts in the closet, and I had to wear the same one as yesterday. Is this the way you take care of the family?"

Ana closed her computer and stood up, looking down at Bill. "I want a job because I want to buy a new car and go on a road trip."

Bill thought he misheard, or perhaps imagined Ana's response, so he tried again, but this time with less conviction. "You don't need a job. We're doing absolutely fine financially. You have access to all our money so why do you want a job?"

"I want to buy a new car and go on a road trip. To find myself," she added. "We shouldn't be having this conversation in front of the kids, Bill. Girls, please go in the other room. Your father and I have something to discuss."

The girls picked up their plates and hurried to the living room, delighted by their unexpected good fortune in being able to eat pizza in front of the TV. When the door closed, Ana went and sat next to Bill. She didn't want to have an argument. She wanted Bill to understand.

"Sweetheart, I love you and the girls more than anything. You know that, right? I have dedicated my life to our family. You all came first in my life and I never asked for anything in return. But now the girls are grown up. Soon they will leave, and you have your work and your hobbies. I feel lost, without a purpose, useless. I need to find myself. I need to reinvent Ana." She trailed off. Was she getting through to him? Bill had walked over to the fridge and was rummaging for something to eat. "Bill, Bill please listen to me," she pleaded. He came back to the table and fixed her with the blue eyes she once fell in love with. They looked cold and disinterested.

"I should probably tell you then, since your brought it up. I've been very unhappy recently. I don't love you anymore and there is someone else in my life." Then, with deadening simplicity, he said, "I want a divorce."

Ana felt like she had been hit with a hammer between the eyes. Her thoughts started swarming around her like bees who had lost their queen. She was surprised to find that the only part of her that did not feel pain was her heart. Lost for words, she willed herself to not breakdown and cry. She needed to keep her wits about her, to change his mind. Not knowing what else to say or do, she walked over to the fridge and started pulling out random ingredients and putting them on the kitchen counter.

"I'll make you a chicken stir fry. Just how you like it." She went on fixing his dinner with a manic energy. Maybe if she didn't look up and made his dinner quickly, he would forget what he just said, and everything would be the same again. On some deep level, she knew that this was nonsense, and that what had been said could not be taken back.

Bill came over, took the pan out of her shaking hand and set it on the counter. "Ana, listen to me. I want to leave you. I'm suffocating in this marriage. I met someone else and I'm in love with her." He spoke to her slowly and clearly, like one speaks to a slow-witted child.

"Let me fix you your dinner," was all Ana could say. She clung on to this thought as if it was a talisman that would keep Bill under their roof.

"I'm not hungry anymore. I'm going to get a few things and leave tonight." Then he mumbled, "It's for the best."

"What about the girls? What will you tell them?"

"I will write them a note before I leave. You can explain." Like a coward, Bill would leave her to clear up his mess.

"Once I know where I'm staying, I will have them over and explain in person...in a few days." With that, Bill picked up his iPad and left the room. He had been practicing this, waiting for an excuse, an opening to give him the courage to go through with the final act. With her little revolution she had given him the excuse he was looking for. She heard his footsteps on the staircase. Two steps at a time. After twenty years of marriage, he was relieved, even happy for it to end. She remembered last year when he got his long-awaited promotion. She was upstairs folding the laundry when he heard him opening the front door. Without taking his coat off he ran up the stairs to tell her his good news. He picked her up and twirled her around, planting a passionate kiss on her lips. Where had all the love gone?

She could hear him opening and closing doors upstairs, probably looking for a big enough suitcase. Her natural instinct was nudging her to go and help him, or at least inform him that the big grey Samsonite that he was looking for was in the garage on the top shelf. Of course, she didn't, but she found the thought interesting and disturbing in equal measure.

How could she not have seen this coming? When did he stop loving her? Was it the summer before, when he became absentminded and obsessed with his appearance, or was it when he stopped asking her opinion on what wear? That must have been the time. When new, expensive clothes started appearing in the laundry basket. Clothes that she had not seen before. Cashmere jumpers, silk shirts, and boxer shorts that she knew cost thirty-five pounds a pair. At the time, she put it down to a mild midlife crisis. Not the sort of midlife crisis that other husbands had, where they bought sports cars and left their families. A little one. One that would pass. She said nothing to him and congratulated herself on her insight and maturity. Bill was a loving husband and a sensible man.

She was certainly no stranger to the male midlife crisis. Ana had spent many evenings on her sofa comforting sobbing middle-aged women. Women that looked just like she did right now. Ruffled, incredulous, terrified about facing a future on their own. While she whispered encouragement to her friends, she had a strong conviction that this could never happen to her. Bill was a sane and dependable man, and his devotion to his family was his one distinguishing characteristic. They were an unbreakable unit. Of that she had been sure. What else had she been sure about?

Bill appeared at the kitchen door holding a small suitcase and a large blue IKEA bag. "I am going now," he announced, without looking at her. "I'll be in touch in the next few days." With that, he turned around and walked out of the house, out of their lives. After twenty years she was discarded, swept aside like a toy that had come to the end of its useful life. Her home had become a husk and her world had ended.

She tried to cry, but the tears refused to come. She only had a pounding, piercing headache and a deep sense that like Alice she had fallen down a rabbit hole where everything was distorted and unreal.

Chapter Twelve

Wall Street, 1987

Ana and Julie fell in love with New York City instantly. Within a week of arriving, and with the Blazer on its last legs, they found a large one bedroom flat on 44th Street between 10th and 11th Avenue, in what was affectionately called Hell's Kitchen. The girls traded neighbourhood safety for flat size. The bedroom could easily accommodate two single beds and the large built-in wardrobe had plenty of space for the both of them. A paravane that Julie found at a charity shop in East Village separated the room into two equal areas and gave them each a bit of privacy. They would have preferred a two bedroom, but their entry-level salaries meant that they couldn't afford it. They signed a one-year lease, expecting that their annual bonuses would help them move to a bigger flat in a year's time.

Hell's Kitchen could generously be described as *edgy*, but it certainly bore the signs of its violent history. The most common story traces its name to Dutch Fred, a veteran police officer who was patrolling with his rookie partner on West 39th Street near 10th Avenue. They stumbled upon a street riot and his partner commented, "This place is hell itself." Fred responded, "Hell's a mild climate. This is Hell's Kitchen," so the name stuck. They wanted to keep the Blazer for weekend outings, but even one month's parking in the city cost more than the car was worth, so to Julie's dismay Ana convinced her to sell it.

Coming from laid-back California, Ana found New York to be fast and hectic. Every morning, a sea of commuters from Brooklyn and Long Island arrived at Grand Central Station. The army of black and blue suits descended into the bowels of New York to take the subway to Wall Street. The trick was to go with the flow. They both had three weeks before their management rotation program was due to start at Silverman Brothers, so they took the time to explore their new exciting home.

There was so much going on; parties, designer sample sales, around-the-clock events, and of course networking. Ana loved networking with this new shiny breed of people. Clever, successful, and fast talking, they were her kind of crowd. She loved verbal sparring, and in New York she could engage in the sport to her heart's content. The best and the brightest financial minds congregated in the small area south of 14th Street, and soon Ana would be one of them. The prospect made her dizzy with excitement. She had made it at twenty-four. How many people can say that? How many women from her hometown of Woking had made it to the top of the totem pole, in New York, ever?

Her school mates had set their sights much, much lower. Her parents were understandably very proud of their accomplished daughter and Ana puffed up like a peacock whenever she thought of that. During her annual trips back home, she made sure that everyone tracked her progress and knew about her achievements. To be fair, even if she had kept a more modest approach, her mum didn't. She went around their small town with Ana's latest letter in her handbag and read bits of it to whoever casually asked about her and what she was up to in America.

With her money dwindling, Ana resolved not to ask for any more help from her dad and instead took a job handing out towels and signing in guests at an aerobics studio not far from their flat. They let her work out for free off-peak and paid her enough to cover her rent and food shop. Their tiny budgets didn't prevent the girls from having an active life.

They regularly crashed parties at bars and clubs by claiming very tenuous connections to the hosts and munched on canapés at gallery openings. Because there were so many gallery openings every evening, they never had to spend money on dinner. Often, they stuffed enough food in their elegant but roomy bags to cover the next day's lunch too. They met an endless stream of interesting people, and soon they were attending parties and events on a nightly basis. Life in New York was an endless party, and everybody seemed to be spending the kind of money that Ana had only ever seen in films.

There was alcohol, but also drugs. Lots of drugs. Ana was curious but also apprehensive. She probably never would have had the courage to snort, eat, or smoke what was offered had it not been for Ian. Ian was tall and sophisticated in his tailored suit. Fast talking and extremely well bred and well read, he stole Ana's heart the very first time they met at a loft party in Tribeca. Ana was invited by a friend of a friend, and as she mingled amongst the *in* crowd, trying hard to appear at ease, she saw him mixing a drink, with a cigarette hanging from his perfect mouth. She made a beeline for the bar, and without hesitating she leaned over and tried a well-rehearsed line. "This looks interesting, what is it?" Before he had a chance to answer she said, "Can you make me one too?"

Ian looked her up and down. He appreciated what he saw, so he reached for another glass. "Take this one, I will make myself another."

Ana wasn't shy and this was the eighties after all, so when Ian asked her if she wanted to go somewhere quiet, she quickly agreed. They took a taxi to the Upper West Side and walked the last couple of blocks to Ian's building. In the flat, Ian brought out a large wooden box, set it carefully on the coffee table, and lifted the lid.

"Now, Ana, what is your preference?" He picked up two blue pills, put one on the table in front of Ana, and then put the other one in his mouth. "You will like this one," he said.

Ana wanted to know what it was, but she didn't want to appear unsophisticated. She took the little pill between her two fingers and swallowed it without hesitation. Her heart was beating fast, but she hid her nervousness by making small talk. Ian made them two vodka tonics and they sipped their drinks while discussing fiscal policy. An hour passed and Ana felt nothing. Maybe drugs didn't affect her after all. Whatever it was, it wasn't working. But within the next half hour, she changed her mind. She soon found out that she couldn't stand still. She wanted to dance, and humanity had a warm glow that she had never felt before. Ian put on some music and Ana swayed to the rhythm, holding her drink in one hand and a cigarette in the other. She felt wonderful and full of energy. She couldn't stand still! Ian must have felt the same way, because he asked if she wanted to go dancing. It was three in the morning. Where would they go? Ana was puzzled. She had not seen any clubs that stayed open after two.

Ian took her on an unforgettable journey of New York's secret places, magical and mysterious clubs hidden behind plain and discretely guarded doorways. Ana moved through the pulsing crowds as if in a dream. With Ian by her side she danced, laughed and talked for hours. She was having the best time of her life! When they finally emerged, Ana was amazed to discover that the sun was well up in the sky. She had been dancing for ten hours.

As the drug wore off, she wondered about the state of her makeup and hair. She must look dreadful. Ian clearly didn't think so, because he guided her into a taxi and took her back to his flat. Then he made slow, endless, delicious love to her. After, he gave her another blue pill before they showered, and without any sleep or feelings of tiredness, they went out to lunch. Ana was amazed to discover that she still had an enormous amount of energy. She skipped on the sidewalk and, with Ian by her side, they walked all the way to one of Midtown's trendy restaurants. She wasn't hungry though. She had two Bloody Mary's and picked at her omelette. She felt wonderful.

Ana got home late that Sunday afternoon and collapsed on the sofa in front of the TV. Her last thought before finally passing out from exhaustion was that she loved drugs and she wanted to feel that way again. She woke up with a jolt when she felt something touching her nose. Opening her eyes, she saw Julie, holding something against her face. It was their makeup mirror. The image could easily be described as the worst reflection of her face she had ever seen. Right then and there, she decided that as good as drugs made her feel, the way they made her look was simply unacceptable. She asked Julie to remind her of how she looked that morning should she ever decide to take drugs again. It wasn't the possibility of death that scared her, because Ana didn't believe in her own death. It was the damage to her looks that was intolerable.

Ana started her new job a week after Julie. They both walked to the Port Authority and from there took either the E or the A train, and it was a thirty-minute ride to the World Trade Centre. Neither of them liked the New York subway. It was crowded and dingy compared to the one in London. But they needn't have worried, because they both lost their jobs within two months of starting.

It was a Monday like any other when Ana, with a slight hangover, arrived at her desk at Silverman Brothers. She was on her second rotation of the trainee programme at the trading desk. Unlike the investment bankers of the first rotation, who worked well into the night, traders were much more fun once the markets closed, but also unwilling to spend much time explaining things to Ana. They were busy, loud, and making lots of money for Silverman. A small slip in concentration could cost them their jobs and the firm millions of dollars, so Ana was told to be quiet and observe. She was sat in front of a Quotron machine and a thick training manual. So far, she had been making dummy trades, which were evaluated by the trainer after the markets closed. Her eyes were glued to the screen, which updated continuously as the markets moved.

The trading floor was tense. The markets in Asia started falling the night before and the traders sensed trouble. Sure enough, with the opening bell, the Dow Jones started on a downward trend. The trading floor was buzzing, and the shouting was deafening. Ana couldn't follow what was going on, but she could see that it was unusual. She was sat next to Bob, a senior trader who she could see was selectively buying *bargains*. She could hear him mumbling that today fortunes would be made. Mostly, though, everyone else seemed to be selling. By lunch time, Bob had turned ashen, and even though he had stopped buying hours ago, he was not selling either.

"Got to keep your nerve kid when everyone else is losing theirs," he instructed Ana, but his hands were shaking on the keyboard. Ana's eyes were glued to her flickering machine, where the Dow Jones was down 250 points and dropping without any upticks.

When all was said and done, and the closing bell signalled the end of what was a historically disastrous day, everyone around Ana seemed to be in a daze. Many traders were stooped over their desks, holding their heads in a gesture that looked like they had experienced the worst of catastrophes. Others were on the phone, either to clients or to brokers, quietly relaying the damage to their savings and portfolios. Ana stole a look towards Bob. His face became paler and he didn't seem to be present in his surroundings. None of the trainees fully understood the significance of what had happened that day, but the consequences started stacking up quickly.

On Tuesday, the scheduled trainee lunch was abruptly cancelled, so Ana went out with a junior colleague for a walk and a street hotdog. He seemed unruffled as he pointed out to Ana that what happened the previous day would not affect either of them, because they didn't have any clients. Ana was not so sure. Her MBA had taught her otherwise. Big events always had unexpected ripples, she knew that, but she hoped that her colleague was right in his assessment, for both their sakes. She changed the subject to something more uplifting as they munched on their hotdogs on the way back to the office.

As they approached, they heard sirens and panicked voices. They sped up to see what the problem was, trying to see through the growing crowd of people. There was an area enclosed with yellow tape, and within, a bloody mound on the floor, covered with a grey hospital blanket. It was a body. People die every day, everywhere, but Ana had never been this close to a body, and she was rattled. People were whispering, and from what she overhead, whoever was under that blanket had fallen from the viewing platform on the 48th floor of her building. She stood there gawking at the rusty splatters that fanned out from underneath the blanket until her colleague gently guided her into the lobby.

They made their way to the 41st floor in an otherwise empty lift. As the door slid open, they spotted the backs of several blue uniforms. It turned out that it was one of their guys that had jumped. It didn't take long before she was filled in. The jumper was Bob, the senior trader that she had sat next to. The scale of his losses would have ended his career, and he didn't see a way out of his predicament.

He had chosen to end it all before he had to face the consequences. Ana, still in her twenties, couldn't fathom why anyone would choose such a gruesome end over what was just a job. It would take a few decades, a mortgage, and a couple of consumer loans before Ana fully sympathised with Bob's decision.

Most of the trainees that had started in September received identical letters inviting them to meet up with HR, and without exception, they were reluctantly let go or offered the option to be reassigned to the broker training programme. This reassignment meant that she would be on minimum wage, and this would be a loan rather than a salary. If her commissions started rolling in, she would have to pay it back in small amounts. If she left the firm, the loan would be erased.

Silverman Brothers recruited 120 trainee brokers every single month. As excessive as this seemed to Ana at the start of her training, she soon realised why they needed so many. The trainer warned them that less than one percent of the class would make it to the second year, and the firm expected one single person from each class to become a million-dollar producer. These statistics were intimidating, but Ana steeled herself to be the one broker who made it to the top.

With the training over, they were all assigned to four desk pods in the middle of the *bullpen*. The idea behind the bullpen was that recent hires who joined Silverman at approximately the same time could work together to gain experience more rapidly. As they progressed, they would occupy the few offices that surrounded the bullpen, before finally moving into one of the four corner offices. Each subsequent office was slightly better than the one before and the hierarchy was obvious to everyone. It was a brutal environment. On her first day in the bullpen, Ana was given twenty pages from the telephone book. On her desk she had a Quotron machine and a telephone. Her assigned task was to make three hundred calls a day, a number verified by a system that generated a daily call report for the manager to review. The script was simple:

Good morning/afternoon, this is Ana from Silverman Brothers. We offer a full range of financial products that can help you grow your portfolio. Even though I'm sure you are already working with someone, I would appreciate the opportunity to explain how I can help you maximise your returns with some excellent proprietary investments that we have developed here at Silverman. Will you have time to meet with me next week for a brief 15 to 20-minute introduction? [Pause] Tuesday at 3 p.m. in your office works just fine for me. Thank you for your time. I look forward to meeting with you next Tuesday.

This was supposed to work a treat, and Ana had been drilled to understand that it was a numbers game. The more she called, the more appointments she would get. The more appointments she got, the bigger her client list would be.

Ana soon discovered that she rarely got beyond her firm's name before the potential client put the phone down. People had been burned by the crash, and she began to consider herself lucky that she hadn't fallen victim to it herself. Often, she had to tolerate a torrent of abuse from people, directed at the nameless broker who had ruined their savings. Gradually, the trainees modified their scripts to include a reassurance that their clients had not lost any money during the crash, which was technically true. When this didn't shift the scales in their favour, several of them handed in their resignations. Many others would just dial a number, and then as soon as the call registered they would hang up the phone, without saying anything. The manager was adamant about everyone making three hundred calls a day and the trainees were not allowed to leave until the number had been reached. The small concession the company made to the exhausted trainees was to provide free pizzas for those unfortunates that were still there, dialling away after seven in the evening.

By the end of the first month, half of Ana's class had quit. The leaving parties clogged everyone's diaries, until management banned them for fear that they were discouraging those who remained. Ana was herself rapidly losing the will to live, especially since Julie, who was a casualty of the crash, surrendered her share of the flat and flew back to California to lick her wounds in the family nest. She didn't know it then, but that was the last time she would see Julie. Their closeness evaporated with distance and the passage of time, and they followed their separate paths. Neither had the money to fly across America or the resilience to keep up a regular correspondence. Their relationship soon became irrelevant and fizzled out. It was sad, but Ana was not the sort of girl who looked back. She always found it easy to move on. Julie was the past and belonged to a chapter that was now closed. Her present was New York.

With her reduced salary, Ana couldn't afford the rent. After several failed attempts at finding housemates among her dwindling circle of friends, she had to give up the flat and move to a youth hostel in the Bronx. This made her daily commute both expensive and risky, especially late at night. Ian never called back after that single drug-fuelled twenty-four hours. Ana was hurt by his disappearance and retreated into her emotional shell. Wall Street was quickly becoming unglamorous and Ana, exhausted, started to brush up her CV. She didn't really want to return to the UK but with her dwindling resources she couldn't sustain herself in her current job. The competition for entry-level jobs was brutal, because every opening attracted hundreds of applicants who had lost their jobs after the crash. Feeling homesick, tired, and disillusioned, Ana decided that it was time to give up on this particular dream.

Chapter Thirteen

Broken home, broken dreams

Ana would have liked to sit on the couch and eat bonbons for several weeks, at least until she felt better, but she was also a mother who needed to take charge of the crisis and protect her daughters from the aftermath of Bill's abandonment. Bill wrote a short and completely inadequate message to his daughters, explaining how mummy and daddy cared for each other but didn't love each other anymore and would be happier living apart. This did nothing to help the girls understand what had happened to their close-knit family, and like the blow of a blunt object it left all three of them bruised and numb.

The timing of Bill's departure made Ana feel guilty for what had happened. If she hadn't tried to change the *status quo* of the family, Bill might have stayed. Was it her little outburst and subsequent decision to go back to work that made Bill leave, or had he been looking for an excuse all along? Ana wasn't sure, but her daughters were on her side.

"You have done everything for us. Dad betrayed us. He only thought of himself," they declared.

It felt good to Ana to have her daughters' support. Yet she still felt the need to defend him. He was her husband after all, part of her tribe, her unit.

"Give him a few weeks. Once he realises the full extent of what he's done he'll reconsider and come back. We're all he's got." Them and that new woman. How new was she really? Maybe he's had her for years. How could she have missed this?

In the next few days, Ana, to her surprise, realised that she wasn't missing Bill. Not even a little bit. She was hurt and angry at his betrayal, but a small part of her rejoiced in the freedom she had been granted. For the first time in twenty-two years she was in charge of her own destiny, and she didn't need to convince anyone about anything. Just knowing this made her feel lighter, better.

But she was also worried, specifically about money. She didn't even have her own bank account and only vaguely knew the size of the mortgage on the house. She had left all the financial decisions to Bill and had unquestioningly signed every piece of paper he had put under her nose. They were on the same team after all. Now she could see how stupid she had been. She was sure that she was a co-signer on his expensive car loan, his several credit cards and of course the mortgage. When she next made it to the bank, she discovered that the joint bank account only had two thousand pounds. She frantically called Bill at his office from the bank to let him know, only to be told that this was supposed to last her and the girls for a month, and then he would give them another two thousand. He made it clear to her that he didn't intend to continue depositing this amount indefinitely and she would have to find work as soon as possible.

"The girls are in school all day. There is no reason for you not to work," he snapped at her. "And don't call me at work, I'm very busy."

"What about the mortgage?" Ana was beginning to panic, and what he said next justified this.

"The house needs to go on the market. I can't afford two mortgages and it's too big anyway. I will pay the mortgage while this is going on and I'll deduct the amount from your share of the proceeds."

Ana's knees gave way and she had to hold on to the wall. Her home of seventeen years, her pride and joy, where every item was a piece of herself, was going to be sold? Where would she and the girls live? How could she afford a home on her own? She still owned her flat in Shoreditch, but if they moved back to the city the girls would have to move schools. Also, she needed the rent for living expenses.

"You can't make the girls move. This is their home too."

"I plan to have the girls half of the time, anyway," he announced. "We will have shared custody" With this last word he put the phone down.

Ana's financial worries were subsumed by her love for her children. She didn't care about money if it meant fighting Bill about the girls, who were her life, her everything.

The prospect of shared custody made her realise how insignificant her little revolution had been. The problems of a middle-class housewife who's bored and has nothing else to complain about. What would her life be like away from her daughters for half of the month, in a new home, with nothing to look forward to. She felt sorry for herself and wanted to cry, but she didn't want to do it in public. She made her way to her little Yaris. In the storm of the recent weeks, it seemed strangely comforting and familiar. A refuge from a world that was becoming unrecognisable. That was changing so fast it made her head spin.

She was going to need help. Was there any paperwork about their finances? She ran upstairs to the study and tore through the drawers and neatly labelled folders, looking for bank statements. There were three relevant folders: "Bank", "House", and "Investments." They were all empty. The empty folders told her all she needed to know. Bill had been planning this for months, or maybe years. The speed with which he made arrangements at the bank and got rid of financial paperwork showed a clear method behind what appeared to be a spur of the moment decision. She had been blind and a fool.

A second visit to the bank, with Meghan in tow for support, revealed that Bill had taken a second mortgage on the house, and her signature was there on the paperwork to prove that she had been in agreement. Ana even remembered signing on the dotted line a few months ago. When she was at her busiest, preparing dinner, he put a piece of paper under her nose, mumbling something about getting a lower interest rate. She scribbled her name without giving the form a second look. Even if she sold the house, her share of the proceeds, once both mortgages had been paid, wouldn't be enough to live on. She would need to rent. The uncertainty of her financial future terrified her.

Meghan, with her classical education, was of little help when it came to finances, but just the fact that she was on Ana's side made her feel a little bit better.

"You need to get your CV to a recruiter today, and we need to get you a lawyer. Bill tricked you and a court will understand that. He needs to support you and the kids, plus everything that he owns is half yours."

Meghan kept talking but Ana wasn't listening. She had made up her mind. As soon as she returned home from the bank, she called Bill. "Can we meet up today to start sorting things out please?" she said, in the most reasonable tone that she could muster. "Can you come by the house before the girls come back from school to discuss?" Bill made some noises about being very busy but agreed to stop by. Sorting things out, at least in the way that Bill was hoping, was the furthest thing from Ana's mind.

Ana had a plan. The fog of desperation lifted, and she felt hopeful. She was going to woo him back. They had a long history together. He used to be crazy about her. All she needed to do was start brushing her hair in front of the mirror and he'd stop whatever he was doing to drag her to the nearest bed and tear her clothes off. That wasn't that long ago. She did a quick mental calculation. Actually, the last time she could recall true passion between them was ten years ago. It didn't matter, she could ignite it again. Of that she was quite sure.

She spent the afternoon getting in and out of outfits, frilly underwear and impossibly high heels. Thank god she had done her hair already and it was looking bouncy and shiny again. At the bottom of her makeup bag she found the red nail polish that used to drive him mad. It was a bit dry, but she put it on nevertheless. At last she was ready, and every mirror in the house confirmed that she looked good. She was a bit on the chunky side, but this never bothered him before. His favourite pie was in the oven and a big tub of Ben & Jerry's Chunky Monkey was chilling in the freezer. Her spirits were soaring, and she had her script at the ready.

Bill arrived twenty minutes late and he formally rang the doorbell. Ana looked out of the window and saw his car parked on the street. There was someone in the passenger seat. A woman, looking at her phone. She couldn't quite make her out, but she was undeniably very young and looked quite slim. Ana felt deflated and self-conscious. Was she the competition? Why did he bring her here? She made her way to the door, feeling a bit silly and overdressed. The man on the doorstep looked younger and decidedly happier than a few weeks ago. His hair looked different and it suited him. He wore low slung jeans, a black V-neck jumper—cashmere, she speculated—and a fitted blazer. He didn't seem like her husband anymore. The woman waiting in the car must have picked his clothes and hairstyle, moulded him into a new man. Bill couldn't even pick his own boxer shorts. Face to face with her rival's influence, Ana's confidence slipped away.

What happened next was swift and brutal. He refused a drink and she realised that he wouldn't be eating his favourite pie either. It probably wasn't even his favourite anymore. She guessed that the girl in the car was feeding him sushi, champagne and strawberries. What a fool she had been! She wondered whether it was even worth trying. He wasn't even looking at her. His sole purpose was to tie up any loose ends and move on with his new life. Ana was smart enough to see that.

As soon as Bill realised there was no quick resolution on offer, he couldn't wait to leave. "I have someone waiting in the car," he informed her. "When you're ready to discuss divorce terms, message me. Just remember that time is running out. I have hired an agent for the house. His name is James and he will be calling you soon to arrange a valuation. Make sure that the house is in order and looking at its best. For both out sakes."

Ana stood in her high heels and short dress in the middle of her own living room, listening to her husband's instructions about how he was going to cut her off and make her and their children homeless. There was no warmth, love, or even plain decency left in him. She was on her own. In what she later came to bitterly regret, Ana begged him to come back. She collapsed in front of him, tears streaking down her cheeks. Holding on to his new blazer, she wailed in a voice that she didn't recognise as her own. "Please Bill, don't do this. Don't break up our family. What are we going to do without you? The girls are desperate." What she said last was not entirely true. The girls had got on with their lives without much fuss, but they didn't know that soon they were going to be thrown out of their home.

Ana despised herself for begging him, but she despised herself even more for having been so trusting and stupid. She pleaded for him to return not because she loved him, or because she wanted his company, but because she had ceded all financial control to him and had no way to support herself if he stopped paying the bills. She fell victim to the same trap that countless women have willingly put themselves into. She wanted to open the window and scream to every mother out there, pushing a pram, that her life was in danger. She wanted to warn them to go back to work as soon as possible, have their own bank account and take care of themselves, things that she had planned to do when she first got married to Bill. Instead she had spent a lifetime, eighteen years, raising babies, toddlers and moody teenagers, cooking, cleaning, and taking care of everyone's needs but her own. Ana realised how little she had got in return, even without this final rotten insult.

After he was gone, she kicked off her heels, took off the uncomfortable dress that barely fit her anymore, and removed her makeup. She felt ashamed for her role in the scene that had just happened. She used to be the girl that every man wanted. She had it all. She was funny, smart, attractive, and had a great job. But look at her now. She was unwanted, on top of the rubbish pile. A fat, worn out housewife begging a man for his support. And not any man! A despicable cheat, a disloyal and cruel stranger, whose socks she had paired for the better part of her life. Ana stopped herself. The girls would be home soon, and she didn't want to drag them into her despairing world. She set the table and became the mother they were expecting to see when they walked through the door.

Chapter Fourteen

A friend in need

All her friends had been conspicuously absent throughout the drama of the last few weeks. Meghan was the only one who called every day to make sure that she was alright, and the only one who brought tissues and wine. She comforted the girls and offered financial assistance to the broken family. Even though Ana declined to take money from her friend, it was great to feel supported and cared for.

As Ana climbed out of the black mood she had been in, she picked up the phone and called Jane, a close friend. The two of them had been inseparable for over a decade and Ana felt slightly embarrassed to have left her out of the loop of what was happening in her life. At the root of her delay was the verbal lashing she would get. Ana hadn't felt strong enough to face Jane's loving judgements about what had gone wrong in her marriage, so she had waited.

The voice at the other end of the phone was cold and detached. Ana thought that her friend may have thought she was someone else, that somehow the events of the past few weeks had made her voice unrecognisable. But no. Jane knew who was calling and she didn't want to hear from her. During the call, Jane made excuses as to why she couldn't meet, and Ana realised that she had lost a friend, if she was ever one to begin with.

Meghan, wonderful Meghan, was always there for her. Jane, on the other hand, had shown her the ugly consequences of divorce. Suddenly, like Jane, many of the women in Ana's life withdrew completely and she was no longer invited to any of their events. Ana didn't understand, but Meghan knew.

"They're afraid about their husbands. Single women are always a threat to women in relationships. They're also afraid you'll ask them for money, and they're not sure what to say to you about the divorce. I'm afraid sweetie that you are out of the circle of trust. Our suburb has no space for divorced women." Meghan had a long sip from the wine she had brought and topped up Ana's glass. "Fuck them," she concluded, "you have me, and I'll always be there for you."

Ana would have got over her social ostracization had Bill and his new girlfriend been ostracized too. But no, they were being invited to everything. Parties, after-school events, ski trips, picnics. Their mutual friends had taken sides, and they always chose Bill, as if the divorce was all her doing. They forgave his cheating and despicable behaviour and took to punishing Ana. This she couldn't understand, and it hurt deeply.

"It's so unfair! What have I done to deserve this? Even Jane, one of my best friends, has picked him instead of me," she sobbed in Meghan's lap. This betrayal was the one that cut the deepest. Meghan sussed Jane out from the very beginning and finally gave herself permission to tell her friend what she really thought about that pretentious little shit that Ana had given her precious friendship to.

"Jane has always been insincere. You were duped. I always thought there was something vacuous about her." And in true form she added, "fuck her!" The childhood friends looked at each other mischievously over Meghan's profanity and burst out into cleansing laughter.

"Yeah, fuck her and the rest of them," Ana managed between her giggles.

Chapter Fifteen

A warning to the curious

Tidying up was a chore, especially when it wasn't Ana's stuff. At the same time, she couldn't bear messiness, so she felt like Sisyphus, punished by the gods to push a large rock up a steep hill, only to have it roll back down as soon as he reached the top. Every mother is punished like this, unless of course she's willing to shut her eyes to everything children leave in their wake.

Every morning, as soon as the kids were out the door, Ana would venture into the wild west of their bedrooms to make the beds and pick up laundry. Last week, she came across an unassuming black notebook with a scrap of paper peering through its well-thumbed pages. It was partially hidden by Hannah's lime green duvet, a colour she would never have picked herself. Having allowed Hannah to redecorate her room as a birthday present, she couldn't have said no to the ugly duvet. She remembered her bringing it to the till at John Lewis. She said triumphantly, "look what I found Mum! It's the last one they have, and it's on sale." She was hugging it tightly as they left the shop and her happy face made Ana temporarily forget what they had just bought.

She knew that the black notebook was her diary because it said so on the cover. Of course, she would never read her diary—unless she suspected that she was having sex or doing drugs—but the little piece of paper appeared to be a separate thing, hastily shoved between the pages. She didn't want to pull it out in case Hannah had placed it at a specific page in the book, so she kept the diary open while she removed the paper. She briefly considered if her action was an invasion of privacy, but decided that it wasn't.

The paper was a letter. A letter from Bill, who she later found out cheated on her with an intern from his office. She hadn't spoken to him since that embarrassing incident when she was sitting in his car on the driveway, begging him to come back. She had heard from Hannah that his new relationship wasn't going well, and he was thinking of moving out. She said that he was miserable and had gained weight.

Secure in that knowledge, over time she let her anger subside got on with her life. His life without her was shit and he totally deserved it. The letter, however, told her otherwise. Hannah had hidden the truth from her. Bill was going to get married. They were thinking of going to the Maldives for their honeymoon. He loved her and they were blissfully happy. He wanted Hannah to know this and be happy for him.

Her poor baby had lived under the weight of that knowledge and protected her from it. It upset her to hear that Bill had found a life without her. Bill was going to the Maldives with his girlfriend and she would have to carry on her motherly duties. She settled down and looked at the revolting green duvet. She was going to have to change it once Hannah left for university.

Chapter Sixteen

London, 1988

As the 1980s came to a close, Margaret Thatcher's Britain was enjoying a period of booming employment. After her disastrous experience on Wall Street, she wanted a job that kept her close to the markets, but not so close that she could be burned again in such a spectacular fashion. She wanted a job with a regular income, promotions, and civilised working hours. After a few interviews, she was offered a job at the investment department of Midland Standard Bank as a wealth manager, exactly the kind of job she was hoping to score. The title of manager was a bit gratuitous, because she had no one to manage or even the prospect of ever having an underling, but this suited her fine. Ana was an independent worker, a lone wolf. She had determination and talent. But what she did have a shred of, was patience with fools or group working spirit. She simply worked too fast for most people and being put in a situation where she had to convince others of her ideas, she found tedious and exhausting.

Ana managed to progress rapidly, despite her insistence on ignoring most of the conventions that constitute a *good* employee. Her broker experience and international reach gave her an edge that couldn't be found even in some of the more experienced wealth managers, who often came to her for advice. Her performance was outstanding, and she became the shining example within her team. Ana had unshakeable principles that extended to her work life, and it was this unyielding integrity that her clients sensed when they trusted her with their money.

The only thing that wasn't going well was her living situation. Ana was staying with her parents and she found the situation intolerable. Tracy, Ana's sister, had followed her footsteps to America to study, and that left her to shoulder all of their parents worry and absorb all of their love. They were always anxious about her and wanted to know where she was and what time she would be back, forgetting that she was an adult who had been independent for years. Mum didn't say anything, but Ana could sense her disappointment every time she skipped dinner to go out with friends in the city. Gradually the situation became worse and the tension overflowed. Ana would yell at her mother for ironing her clothes or straightening her bed.

It wasn't her mother's mothering that made her mad. It was her mother's surrender to an empty life of servitude, that derived all of its satisfaction from being needed.

"Mum, what will you do with the rest of your life now that we're all grown up?" she would say. "Why don't you sign up for a course or get a job to get you out of the house?"

Her mother would smile at her fiery daughter, proud to have created such an independent and capable woman. During those conversations she would promise to flick through the course brochures that Ana brought home, but they remained untouched. Her mum was content in her daily drudgery and it seemed to Ana that she took out all her pent-up energy on her.

"You work such long hours darling," she would complain. "You're never home for dinner and your daddy never gets to see you. Why don't you bring some of your friends over?"

"Over for a play date mum? I'm twenty-five years old and a manager in a London bank. You need to let go and find something else to do with your life."

These encounters always descended into heated arguments and left Ana feeling angry and guilty in equal measure. She knew the solution. She had to find her own place, and soon.

Chapter Seventeen

Her own home

The housing market in London was heating up and interest rates started to rise. Ana, being a wealth manager, decided that she would put her money where her mouth was and take her first step on the property ladder. Ana had accumulated a small but adequate deposit, and within a few months she was the proud owner of a two-bedroom flat in up and coming Shoreditch. Well, it was actually a one-bedroom flat with a roomy broom closet, but the very small second bedroom had a window and would work well as an office.

Shoreditch was becoming an edgy centre of fashion, with artists renting the shabby flats and turning them into studios. There were trendy cafes, nightclubs, and impromptu raves. Ana absolutely loved her new neighbourhood. The flat was on the second floor of an old Victorian townhouse in desperate need of a face-lift. When Ana finally got the keys, she took a day off work and spent the entire afternoon sitting on the floor, planning her renovation project. She would paint the walls, refinish the hardwood floors, and, with the next commission payment, get a new IKEA kitchen. She was on fire!

Ana wasn't afraid of hard work. For the next several weeks she spent every evening and weekend sanding and painting. She would get home from work, take off her suit, and get stuck into her project, forgetting to have dinner, until the Mickey Mouse clock on the windowsill reminded her that she needed to go to bed. She lived on Indian takeaways, frozen pizzas and ready meals, and slept on a futon on the floor. During this time, Ana understood the meaning of the term "flow." Being totally absorbed in her project, night after night would go by without her noticing. Every morning she would hastily remove traces of paint from under her fingernails and her hair before going to work, and even at work, her heart lay with her paint bucket at home.

One evening, her project was finally finished. Ana ordered Thai takeaway, lit a candle, poured a glass of wine, and sat on her futon in a state of utter happiness. After years of pushing around intangible assets and never really creating anything concrete, here was something solid and beautiful. How remarkable to feel such pure joy over a home improvement project. She reflected on her career choice, and she did this more often as the stress of her job increased. It was only that steadily increasing stream of income that kept her chained to her desk and the long hours she had to put in.

The new improved flat was a daily source of pride and joy for Ana. Her parents, concerned about the lack of a proper bed, contributed much of the furniture. The rest of her stuff was cobbled together from charity shops. During her project she had rejected all invitations and had barely seen any of her friends. With the flat completed, she embarked on a whirlwind of social engagements, with a common theme of always beginning or ending with a drink in her bohemian living room. Ana hadn't been afraid to mix and layer colours and patterns. She created a space that was beautiful, unconventional and comfortable, that soon made her *cool* amongst her circle of friends.

Ana relished the reputation, despite inwardly believing that it wasn't justified. She often felt like a fake. It was a secret that she kept buried deep inside her. She supported all of the trendy *causes* that appeared in the news or were discussed amongst her friends and at work. Every now and again she would even contribute financially to these causes, especially in public view. In truth, however, she knew that she didn't really care and wondered whether others felt the same as she did. Was her coolness a fraud? She had a style of her own and didn't need to follow anyone or conform, but she often took someone else's style or idea and made it her own. Did this count? She didn't know, but she still enjoyed the admiration.

Chapter Eighteen

Love at work, a bank romance

Ana was promoted to senior manager, and she got to share an assistant with a man a decade older than her, called Clive. He sat across from her in a premium window-facing cubicle, assigned to them in recognition of their senior status. Most of the day he would be hunched over the phone talking to his clients, lightly tapping on his keyboard. Between phone calls he sometimes leaned over the grey divider between their two desks to ask her if she wanted a cup of tea. Sometimes he passed a mint or a cookie from a jar he hid in his desk drawer. The only picture on his desk was that of a shaggy dog, chewing on a tennis ball.

Clive was a good-looking guy, with a full head of hair and what looked like a fit body under his crisp shirt. Ana sort of fancied him, but she was reluctant to take it further. His twinkling blue eyes and wicked sense of humour made her wonder whether she should, and he showed real joy at her successes. He seemed genuinely happy for her, something that she hadn't encountered before in the cutthroat environment of Wall Street.

Clive, like many others in the city, started as an apprentice to a broker straight after he finished his GCSEs, and despite his lack of formal qualifications, he had a natural talent for understanding his clients' needs and finding the best way to help them. He often came to Ana for advice and she was happy to give it. In return, he often bought her drinks and occasionally dinner after work. Ana enjoyed their uncomplicated relationship. They were work buddies.

But during one drunken evening, Ana made up her mind to give it a go and become more than a colleague. Ana knew that relationships at work were always bad news, but she didn't see her infrequent romps with Clive as a *relationship*. More like recreation. Her mum would have been appalled, but this was the late 80s and the world was a much more understanding place for women.

In truth, Clive fulfilled almost all of what Ana hoped to get out of a relationship. He was funny, good in bed, willing to go out at a moment's notice and very presentable. He also made minimal demands of her, and they had some delightful romps after hours when the office was deserted.

Ana liked that she felt fully in control of the relationship. She had no patience for women who would pine, cry or otherwise humiliate themselves over a guy. Her standard advice to her friends was always, "plenty more fish in the sea," or, if she was feeling charitable, "when one door closes another one opens." It never occurred to her than a man could have the sort of power that could turn a woman into a bawling wreck. She found this to be pathetic and weak. She didn't believe in romantic love, at least not the kind that makes someone take leave of their senses.

Ana's advice was well sought after. Her down-to-earth manner and unwavering loyalty made her a fabulous shoulder to cry on. Her sensible and practical tips empowered her friends to reach for more than they thought themselves capable of. Whether it was guys, property, or jobs, she made it clear that everything was possible if they only tried, and Ana knew the method and had the tools. Her bedside manner was not for the fainthearted, but those who listened to her told her that it worked, which made her a bit of a legend when it came to wholesale restructuring her friends' lives.

Clive was oblivious to all these machinations, and like most guys he was just happy to be with a pretty girl. Their relationship was based on friendship and camaraderie. They weren't prone to jealous rages, tears, or commitment demands. Occasionally (and privately) Ana pondered about the lack of drama in her relationship with Clive, and even wondered whether their sex life would be better if they argued a bit. But overall, she was happy with what she had, and she felt smug when she compared her love life to that of her friends.

"Love is a myth," she lectured to any female who would listen. "The most important thing in a relationship is to be friends and have compatible interests." Her friends would nod in agreement and then, to Ana's dismay, continue to meet and date unsuitable men.

Every now and again, Ana would take on one of her friends as a project. She would pick the most hopeless cases and advise them relentlessly on how to land a serious boyfriend or husband. She had a strong belief that women had been tutored wrongly and it was her purpose in life to set them straight and make them strong and resilient. Her romance continued to flourish, and with that box ticked she could fully concentrate on her career.

Chapter Nineteen

Here comes Michael!

I liked being with him, as I like being with swift animals who are motionless when at rest.

— Colette, The Pure and the Impure (1932)

Clive and Ana celebrated their two-year anniversary of successful and uncomplicated dating with an expensive dinner at a restaurant not far from the office. Things were going well, and Clive had asked her a couple of times to consider moving in together. Between the two of them they would be able to afford a much better place and Ana was starting to come around to the idea. Clive had been housetrained from years of living alone and would not expect her to wait on him hand and foot like Thomas had. She wasn't interested in marriage, as she found the concept obsolete, but living together made sense.

She was still mulling over the idea of committing to Clive, but one day, she stumbled on Love with a capital

"L." She took a full-on nosedive into its depths that she never felt was possible.

Michael Hale was powerful. With his rugged good looks, he could have been the hero of the steamiest of romance novels. He ran the bank's investment division and at thirty he was the youngest person ever to do so.

Michael came to the bank's investment training session to drum up interest in his division's offering. At the drinks reception that followed the presentation, Ana was introduced to him as the top salesperson in the wealth management department. Even though she didn't believe in love at first sight, Ana was forced to admit the error of her ways when she set her eyes on Michael.

Michael was a married man, and Ana was now seriously involved with her boyfriend, but none of this seemed to matter. After flirting wildly during the party, she followed him to a hotel, where they stayed for the next twenty-four hours, ignoring their phones and the increasingly desperate messages from both Clive and Michael's wife. Ana felt like she was in a parallel universe and this sense of unreality continued in the coming weeks. She unceremoniously broke up with Clive, and Michael arranged for her to be transferred to another division of the bank.

Uncharacteristically, Ana was at Michael's beck and call, asking for nothing more than to be near him. At her desk she would recall their frantic couplings and fantasise about their future together. Michael was often unable to meet her, but even on those days she didn't go out with her friends, just in case his plans changed. On rare occasions he was able to stay the night, but most times they just met at her flat right after work, or even during lunch times.

Even though at some level Ana knew that it was wrong to sleep with another woman's husband, she felt powerless to stop it. Michael told her that his marriage had been a mistake and that he had never loved his wife the way he loved her.

"Soon I will ask for a divorce, and we will be together forever," he would promise before he headed back to the office after a lunchtime quickie. Ana believed every word.

Soon she had no social life at all, because she had been sworn to secrecy until the divorce. Her friends eventually stopped calling, and Ana spent her evenings writing in her diary and getting drunk on her own. Her performance at the bank also suffered, but nobody reprimanded her. Ana suspected that her affair was not as secret as Michael thought and that her manager was not about to mess with his boss' girlfriend. In a rare moment of self-reflection, Ana realised that she had become a *mistress*, the kind of woman she loathed. But it never occurred to her to feel bad about wrecking Michael's marriage. His wife was a faceless obstacle, and in those pre-internet days she had no way of finding out anything about her. Whenever she pushed Michael for details, he avoided her questions and swore to her that none of that mattered because he would soon leave his wife to be with her.

It took two phone calls for Ana to be shaken out of her stupor. The first was from a woman in the middle of the night.

"You better be careful," said the voice in a raspy whisper. "Do you know where he is tonight?" Before Ana had a chance to say anything the woman hung up. Ana stood there, shivering in her nighty, holding the buzzing phone before deciding to find out. She knew his home number. With trepidation, she dialled it. Surely, at two in the morning, he would be at home. Why would he be anywhere else? The phone rang a few times before a sleepy female voice answered it. Ana quickly hung up. She waited a few minutes and called back. The same voice answered. This was getting her nowhere so she went back to bed, but she couldn't sleep. Sick with worry and full of suspicion, she laid there tossing and turning until it was time for work.

As soon as she arrived at the bank, she went straight into Michael's office and told him about the call the previous night. She omitted telling him about her calls to his house and waited to see if he brought anything up. He didn't. Michael assured her that he had been at home, fast asleep in the guest bedroom and that the person who called her must have been a prankster fishing for gossip. She wanted to believe him, so she did.

The second call, a few weeks later, was harder to ignore, and brought her world crashing down. It was from his wife. Like every other mistress before her, she found out that Michael was happy at home and had no intention of leaving his wife. The wife had known about and forgiven previous indiscretions and she would also forgive this one. Michael was her husband and Ana was one of several mistresses that meant very little to him.

Ana dismissed the call as the ravings of a jealous woman, but when she asked Michael his eyes told her what she needed to know. He looked like a dear caught in the headlights, and the only thing he managed to say in response was, "Fuck." In a scene that she replayed in her head many times with deep embarrassment, Ana begged him to stay. Almost in hysterics, she held on to his shirt, burying her face into his chest.

"It's for the best that she knows," she wailed.

But he pushed her to the ground. "You know nothing of me or my wife, you little slut," he barked. "Did you tell her? How did she find out?" Ana desperately protested her innocence, but he didn't stick around to hear her out. Like that, he was out of Ana's life.

A lucky break

Ana needed money and she needed it fast. She would need to get a lawyer if she had any hope of a good settlement, not to mention all her other expenses. Was there anyone who would take a chance on her? She wasn't sure. Banking was the territory of the young. When she went to her first interview, coincidentally with someone who used to be an intern at her old job, she couldn't spot many people her age, and of the ones she saw, none were women. Was it because they had all given up on work, or had work given up on them?

The job was a simple one at the bank's customer-facing desk, answering inquiries, opening new accounts, and helping reset pins on bankcards. It was the type of job that would become obsolete in the next ten years the way things were going with technology, but it was available now and that was all that mattered. She had to start somewhere.

The interview was at the 40th floor of one of the new towers that dominated the city. Ana hardly recognised Sally, her old intern, who sat behind an impressive desk tapping on her sleek laptop. There was nothing else on the desk, not even a single piece of paper. It must have been a new policy. She had read somewhere about banks going paperless and wondered whether she should give Sally the paper copy of her CV she had brought along. She decided against it.

"Welcome! So great to see you!" Sally walked around the big desk and gave Ana a hug.

"Thank you so much for agreeing to see me." Ana was surprised by the warmth in her voice.

"You were such a legend around the bank. I couldn't believe my luck when I got your call. It's impossible to hire capable people these days. I think they teach them nothing at school. Many can't string a sentence together, let alone write."

Ana smiled at the thought of her daughters and the cryptic messages they exchanged with their friends. "Yes, your right, this new generation has simplified communication a lot. You need a dictionary to understand all their abbreviations. Hopefully they'll know enough not to carry it through to their professional lives."

"Oh, but they do," lamented Sally. "We get complaints all the time, and what's worse is that they refuse to pick up the telephone, as if it will bite them. Everything is by email and email can come off as rude or uncaring sometimes. We get a lot of complaints."

Listening to Sally, Ana felt a bit better about her prospects. At least she could write full sentences and had no problem picking up the phone.

Sally went on. "I brought you in for the customer service job in the retail banking department, but I also have something else in mind. I'm looking for a sales assistant. Someone to deal with first line inquiries and take some of the pressure off me. How would you feel about working for your old intern?"

Ana thought about that. Would it be weird? She decided that there was nothing about Sally today that reminded her of the shy and awkward girl that made her coffee a few decades ago. "I would love to be your assistant Sally," she said. "I've signed up for a few evening courses to catch up with developments and I'm really excited about getting back to work. Like I told you on the phone, even before Bill left, I started preparing my CV. With the girls grown up, I felt like I'd lost my purpose."

"You? The amazing Ana? Lost her purpose?" Sally looked stunned. "You were the most determined woman I have ever met. Once you had your goal in sight, you were like a steamroller. Nobody at the bank ever got near your sales numbers. You just had a bad break. I'm sure that you will find your old self once you're back at the office."

Ana hoped that Sally was right. The person she was describing must still be somewhere inside her, even though Ana hardly remembered her. Is it possible that she had changed so much as to be unrecognizable even to herself?

Ana thought about this the whole way home. She tried hard, in the hollows and dells of her memory, to bring back a full picture of what she was like, but all she came up with was a figure made of loose fragments and broken images. The years had changed her dramatically, there was no doubt about that. Her family had changed her. Life had changed her. Gradually, but relentlessly, she had become someone else. Someone's wife, someone's mother. A new feeling arose in her, one of pride for who she had been, but also indignation for who she had become. Then followed anger, searing hot anger, towards Bill. She focused on him and how he had robbed her of her essence. He just took and took and took, and when all was taken, he threw the husk out.

Ana recognised that she was being dramatic, but she didn't care. It was a release to blame him for everything. The loss of her career, her dreams, herself. It was all his fault, she concluded. And with that, she straightened herself, pulled back her shoulders, and thought about how she had impressed Sally. She was still in there.

Chapter Twenty-One

She's back!

Despite any doubts she once had, it took Ana less than two months before she felt at home in her new role. The pay would take a bit of time to catch up, but this hardly mattered. Once she knew that she could do the job and that her sales skills were intact, her confidence grew by the day. Sally was absolutely delighted to have her, and the two of them fell into a routine that suited them both. Ana didn't need any supervision and she only went to Sally when she had questions about procedure and compliance.

During this time, Ana had very little contact with Bill, who, according to the girls, was in a state of blissful happiness with his new girlfriend. All communication was either by email or through the girls, who had taken their parents split in stride and didn't seem particularly upset by the new arrangements. They saw their dad once a week and on the odd weekend when he could make it.

Ana was surprised by how little she missed Bill and her old life. The excitement of being back at work—with other adults who spoke about adult stuff—drowned out any misgivings she had about the collapse of her marriage. In one of their girly chats, she confided to Meghan that she felt happier than she had been in years. Every morning she got out of bed with all the energy she had before the girls were born. Her clothes had gone from being tight and uncomfortable to hanging so loose that Sally commented that they needed to go shopping together.

When the divorce papers came through six months later, Ana signed them without a shred of regret. That era had finished, and even though she resented Bill for his behaviour, she felt that his decision had ultimately benefited both of them.

"Perhaps marriage should be a contract that ends when the kids are out of school," she told Meghan over a bottle of wine. "If the couple are happy together, they can renew it on an annual basis, otherwise it should end without recriminations. Think how much easier it would have been for me if I knew that from the beginning. I would have kept my career and be making more than Bill by now for sure!"

Meghan, who had never considered life without her husband, paused at the thought. "I don't know, maybe. I mean we are very happy, and he is my best friend, but we only have sex a few times a year, and even then, kind of reluctantly. I don't really miss it. I do sometimes wonder what it will be like just me and him once the kids are gone." Meghan hesitated, perhaps thinking that she had gone too far with her private thoughts, but then the wine spoke. "Sometimes, I wonder what my life would have been like if I had never met him. I'm also not one hundred percent sure I would have chosen him again if I had to go back, assuming I could still have my kids."

Ana wasn't surprised to hear this, that her friend had contemplated an alternate future. She too had done it often, but never admitted it to anyone. It seemed to her like an act of betrayal.

Meghan continued. "To think that we only have one life to live, and in that life only forty or so good adult years. Is being with one person and going through the daily drudgery of married life the best way to use that time?" There. She said it.

Ana looked at her friend, astonished. "Sometimes you really surprise me Meghan. I have always been under the impression that you had achieved all you ever wanted in life—good husband, kids, and a wonderful home. You're my closest friend, but I never would have guessed."

Meghan looked at her friend. "Even saying this to you is making me feel disloyal, but it's true. I probably would have chosen a different route." She stopped, and said abruptly, "I don't really want to talk about this anymore, it's making me feel bad."

The conversation didn't make Ana feel bad, but it made her curious, like she needed to explore the idea further. In her early fifties, she was lucky to have found a good job and survived what could have been financial ruin. But what was she doing with her life? Was she making the best use of her time? If she remained healthy, she had another ten to fifteen good years where she could independently live her life. Did she want to spend this time selling financial instruments? What else could she do? And if she did decide to do something different, how could she support herself financially?

Chapter Twenty-Two

An affair with severe consequences

Michael's sudden and traumatic departure ripped Ana's heart to shreds. She knew she had been duped, but she still loved him and couldn't imagine a life without him. She sent him long letters in confidential inter-office envelopes and increased her office hours to make sure that she would run into him several times a day. But it was no use. He had erased her from his life.

A few days later she had to attend her first disciplinary hearing. Her manager wanted to address her declining performance. Sensing that her status had changed and that she was no longer protected, he saw no reason to put up with her dwindling sales and long absences. Following that meeting, Ana tried to pull herself together. She couldn't afford to lose her job and fall behind with her mortgage payments. But also, she was scared that she would lose all contact with Michael.

With Michael out of her life, she realised how many friends she had lost by not returning calls or turning down invitations. Her work colleagues, who had secretly resented her intimacy with the boss, became openly cold and hostile, sensing that her days at the office were numbered.

During the transfer from the old office, she lost her largest accounts, and in her new territory she hadn't made any inroads. She didn't like leaving the office for meetings in case Michael came looking for her, even though he hadn't contacted her in weeks or responded to any of her messages. On some level, she knew that the situation was hopeless, yet she couldn't let go of her obsession, and she hated herself for her weakness.

One day, finally, her luck ran out. In a brief meeting she was let go, and unceremoniously marched out of the office with a cardboard box of her personal belongings. She cried for days. She cried for Michael. She cried out of fear for her future, and above all out of rage for the injustice of it all. Nothing had happened to him. He had his job, his home, and his wife, and would probably date another unsuspecting woman at the office. She had lost everything, and if she didn't pull herself together, she would probably lose her home as well.

Ana managed to extract a reference letter from her manager by implying that she had been let go because of the affair with Michael. Her manager didn't acknowledge her threat but was quick to include a month's wages and the reference letter in her severance package.

With her money running out, Ana took action. It took less than a week for her to get an offer at Gower Long Savings Bank, a fierce competitor of her old employer in the wealth management arena. She didn't let them down. Soon enough, she won them all her old accounts, because her clients missed her no-nonsense approach to investing.

Ana wanted to show her old employer and Michael that they had made a terrible mistake in letting her go. It was a matter of pride, and she had plenty of that.

Ana never quite got over Michael, often referring to him as the love of her life. But she came to understand how she had been taken advantage of by a man who never intended to leave his wife for her, and only saw her as a break from his marital routine. Several months later, she started getting phone calls in the middle of the night. The person would say nothing and then hang up. She was sure it was Michael, but despite the pangs that she still felt thinking about him calling her in a dark corner of his living room as his wife slept upstairs, she did the sensible thing and changed her number. She had learned her lesson and would never make the same mistake again.

Chapter Twenty-Three

Ana goes out and meets a man

Sally was a single lady herself, and despite their age difference, she would often drag Ana out to various events in the city "to meet a guy." Ana found these events boring, and she never fancied the cheap wine and fatty canapés. Most of the guys they met were looking for consulting work or trying to sell recruitment services. She would smile while trying to avoid striking up any conversations, mostly acting as a wingman for Sally.

In no time, Ana found out why Sally was still single. Despite her brilliance at work and professional approach in meetings and with clients, Sally became a silly, cackling girl whenever she liked a guy. After a few glasses of wine, she became loud and obnoxious, and men would give her a wide berth. Sally had no idea what she was doing wrong, so Ana set out to teach her the art of seduction.

With Ana's instruction, things somewhat improved. Keeping Sally away from the free wine, she finally landed a serious date. Ana was delighted, especially because it got her out of attending those boring after-work events. It also got her thinking that it would be nice to land a date for herself, but after years of marriage, she didn't even know where to begin. As a favour to Ana, Sally introduced her to online dating.

Together they created a profile for Ana, putting in the same amount of effort as they would for a big sales presentation. They agonised over photos, hobbies and the main "elevator pitch." They wanted to present Ana as youthful and active, hoping to attract a guy who was prepared to take a chance on a middle-aged, divorced woman with two teenage daughters. Admittedly, not the most attractive package for most guys. The responses Ana got were few and not at all to her taste. She wasn't willing to compromise, so she remained single.

Then, out of the blue, she met the perfect man at a bus stop on the way to work. She recognised him as one of her neighbours, and she had seen him several times before as they took the same bus. They were both late. He looked agitated, and after a couple of minutes of waiting, he gave up and flagged a passing taxi. "Would you like me to drop you off at the city?" he asked Ana, "it's on the way." She agreed and jumped in the back seat with him. It was starting to rain, and she was quite late for her first appointment. "I'm Noel." He put out his hand.

"Ana." She put out hers. "Nice to meet you." In the half hour it took for the taxi to navigate the morning rush hour, they discovered that they were both single, lived within two blocks of each other, and worked in very similar jobs.

Before she got off, he passed her his business card. "Perhaps we can grab a drink after work soon," he said, and

Ana, looking at his wide shoulders and full head of hair, decided that he was worth a chance.

Noel waited a week before he called her, and they agreed to meet for a drink on a night when the girls were staying with their dad. Ana hadn't been on a date for twenty years, but Meghan, who had herself been married forever, was of no help.

"What shall I wear? Should we split the bill? If we hit it off should I let him kiss me? What if he wants to come home with me?" Meghan helped as much as she could but having been out of the dating scene for as long as Ana, her advice was hardly reliable. Ana turned to her daughters for clothes and makeup help, and the girls took on the task with enthusiasm. She also decided to bring cash of different denominations, and even though it appeared very unlikely that things would progress that fast, she also slipped a couple of condoms in her purse.

She met Noel at a trendy city bar. When she arrived, he was already there waiting for her. He looked good in his tailored suit and Ana noticed that several women had their eyes fixed on him. Suddenly she felt very insecure and the dress that looked so good before now felt matronly and unfashionable in this uber chic bar.

Noel spotted her and his eyes lit up. With a drink in her hand and a good-looking man by her side, Ana felt a lot better. So much so, that she had two more drinks in quick succession. The conversation flowed as easily as the drinks, so when Noel suggested dinner, she agreed, even though she wasn't at all hungry. During dinner things sped up considerably. On her way back from the ladies' room, Noel stood up and gave her a passionate kiss. As unexpected as it was, it felt natural, so she kissed him back.

Waiting for the slobbery kiss that she was used to getting from Bill, Ana was surprised to be kissed in a way that made her quiver all over. Noel helped her into her seat and continued with his main course, as if kissing a woman in a way that made her unstable on her feet was something he did every day. By the time they had reached dessert, Ana had made up her mind. When Noel hailed a taxi, she got in without protest. Noel told her that he was taking her to his place and Ana weakly told him that she was not that kind of girl and she wanted to go home.

With a twinkle in his eye, he placed a hand high between her legs and asked if she would rather he stopped. She paused for a moment, and then, throwing away years of her own advice, she spread her legs a little wider and moaned deeply. Hoping the taxi driver wasn't listening in, she leaned over and told him exactly what she wanted him to do to her as soon as possible. He obliged.

That night was quite possibly the most passionate, steamy, and memorable night of her life. She forgot her condoms, her inhibitions, and her twenty years of marriage in one go. With a flick of his fingers he snapped her bra off, and, kissing her deeply, he pinched her nipples until all she could do was open up to him as much as she could, moaning deeply and urgently. When he entered her, she cried out in a voice that she didn't recognise as her own. She begged him to keep going and whispered things in his ear that she had never said to another man.

When Ana slipped out in the morning she wondered if the neighbourhood had heard. It seemed impossible that they hadn't, but nothing stirred as she made her way home a few blocks away. Something about that night had completely erased Bill and all the slights she had suffered from his departure. The skies had opened, and she had been saved. Good sex had saved her. How extraordinary. She lived with someone for decades, had kids together, built a home and a family, and then a night of super good sex comes along and washes it all away.

Chapter Twenty-Four

Bill, then

When Ana met Bill at a work, it never occurred to her that this shy, badly dressed accounts assistant would play such a crucial role in her life. After what had happened with Michael, she had sworn off "fancy" men and work colleagues. Losing her boyfriend and her job at the same time was a big knock, and she didn't want to repeat it. At any other time of her life, Ana would have ignored Bill. He was, how best to say it? Unprepossessing, dependable, a bit dull. All the things that Michael wasn't. If men like Michael should come with warnings, men like Bill should come with instructions that read, "handle with care." This is the best way to describe the difference between the two men.

Bill looked down at his shoes a lot and their courtship began in the most unsexy way. He wanted some kind of a spreadsheet that only Ana could produce. He came asking for it a few times until he finally gathered the courage to ask her out for a drink after work. They would be joining a few people from the accounts department at the pub across the street from the office.

Ana's confidence had taken a beating following her relationship with Michael and the intensity of their affair had lost her more than a few friends. The prospect of meeting new people that didn't remind her of the past was appealing. Bill clearly had little experience with women and Ana found this endearing. When he suggested dinner after the drinks crowd drifted away, she agreed. They split the bill, something that Michael never would have agreed to. But she didn't judge Bill for it. She realised that comparing her potential future boyfriends to a successful executive was unfair. Financially, they would always come up lacking. She understood the perils of the practice, so she paid her share and put the whole thing out of her mind.

Her relationship with Bill progressed steadily and she found that they had a lot in common. They were both very hard working, good with money, and loved the outdoors. Many of their dates involved running, hiking, or biking, followed by a picnic or pub lunch. Their relationship was like a healing balm for Ana, and it progressed at a very slow and unthreatening pace. After several weeks, they had exchanged a few kisses and Bill didn't seem to be in a hurry to ask for anything more than that. In the beginning, this suited Ana just fine. They became friends, something that she never managed with Michael. They talked a lot and made plans for the future, and he proudly introduced her to his friends and family. The lack of sex was a bit puzzling, but not worrying. At that point, she was happy to wait.

Bill came from a large family. He had two brothers and two sisters and what seemed like hundreds of cousins. The family lived in a ramshackle house in the outskirts of Eastbourne, where Bill had grown up. He was a middle child, and even though he was loved, he had been largely left to his own devices growing up. He sometimes let it slip that he had felt a bit neglected when he was young. Whenever he mentioned it, he broke Ana's heart, and she wanted to scoop him up in her arms and cover him with kisses. When she finally met his parents, a lot of things became clear to her. Maeve and Brian had married very young and were barely out of their twenties when the first baby came along. At Ana's age, they had already had four kids, with a fifth one on the way. No wonder Bill had felt neglected.

Bill had a strange relationship with his older brothers. He admired them and desperately wanted their approval, but they mostly ignored him with because of his limited ambitions and modest lifestyle. He was closer to his youngest sister Barbara, a spoiled and conceited girl who Ana disliked from the get-go.

From what Ana could tell, the two of them had formed an alliance of sorts where Bill indulged her and she borrowed money from him that she never returned. Bill was extremely careful with money, almost stingy, so lending money to his sister was his way of showing affection. Ana decided to stay well clear of their relationship and avoided giving any indication of what she really thought of Barbara. Likewise, she stayed tight lipped when Barbara asked about Bill. She sensed that she was jealous of her brother's first serious girlfriend and Ana didn't want to fan the flames. Barbara was hard to like, but Ana made an effort for the sake of Bill.

In the meantime, the lack of sex was beginning to bother her. It was two months into the relationship. He would sleep over but make no effort to do anything more than kiss her. Ana wasn't sure about how to progress, and she sensed that he was very nervous about sex. She began to wonder whether she was his first, which would made him a rare and unusual twenty-nine-year-old virgin. Ana found that thought surprisingly sexy. Be someone's first? How peculiar. Sexy underwear, suggestive talk, running her long red fingernails down his back. Nothing worked.

She finally resorted to the age-old courage-enhancing trick of getting him drunk. Not so drunk that he would pass out, but drunk enough to forget his inhibitions. This finally worked, of sorts. It was a very brief and disappointing encounter, but it was a start. Ana considered it a victory and, as it turns out, so did Bill. He technically hadn't been a virgin. It was his third time. But Ana sincerely wondered whether the other girls had broken up with him because of the bad sex. She steeled herself and decided to give Bill some time to get over his hang-ups and up his game in bed, which he eventually did.

He never became a stallion, and Ana had to fake it on a regular basis, but the sex was tolerable, and she really liked Bill's other qualities, so she stuck it out. In a moment of intimacy, he admitted to her that he had issues with sex, but he didn't clarify further, and Ana didn't probe so as not to hurt him.

As the relationship became more serious, Ana introduced Bill to her friends and family, and they started talking about moving in together. Bill was sleeping under someone's raised bed, with a mattress on the floor and two makeshift shelves of books. He was very near to the office, which was the only saving grace of this arrangement. She almost felt like a saviour when she made their relationship *official* and helped Bill move his few possessions into her flat.

He was delighted with his new surroundings, but he never offered to share in any of the household expenses. Ana didn't know what to make of this but was too embarrassed to ask him to contribute, so she put it out of her mind and made him buy her dinner on a regular basis. She could tell that he didn't like spending money, but it was her way of making her point when it came to finances.

When Bill proposed, he didn't have a ring, nor did he promise one in the future. Ana pretended that she didn't care about a ring but found it hard to explain to her friends why she didn't have one. She resorted to saying that she didn't want one and that she preferred him to use the money for something more practical. Debby liked Bill, but when she found out about the ring, she warned her daughter about planning her future with a cheap guy. Ana jumped to Bill's defence and retorted that it was better to be with a guy with savings than one with debt. Debby kept the rest of her thoughts and reservations to herself. She had a wedding to plan after all.

Chapter Twenty-Five

Everything is not enough

Ana had landed on her feet. She had picked up her career almost where she had left off twenty years earlier. Her finances were in shape and she had a great boyfriend. Her figure had returned to its pre-kids size, helped by regular visits to the gym and eating simple meals on the go. The girls were getting on nicely, almost untouched by the drama of the divorce. All the pieces of total satisfaction with life were there, and for several months Ana convinced herself that she had all that her heart desired.

Her romance with Noel fizzled out, but he was still available to show her a good time at least once every fortnight. Their spark was bright in the bedroom only, and Ana was fine with that. She didn't want to shoulder another man's needs so soon after finding her freedom. This time it was going to be all about her.

Going through a major life upset had changed her. As the framework of her married life disintegrated, Ana saw her universe expand. Suddenly, a lot more was possible, and she realised that it wasn't necessary to limit herself to rebuilding what she had already achieved in her twenties and thirties. One by one the boundaries she had raised for herself toppled and began to fall. Where she was going to live, what kind of work she was going to do (if any), the house that she cherished so much, and the social approval she desired were all flexible and fluid. The realisation came to her in the shower and hit her with force. All was suddenly very clear. She didn't need to spend the next twenty years—maybe all that she had left—preparing for the future. The future had come to her. It had arrived, and she had to discover how to take full advantage of its boundless freedom.

Ana quickly wrapped a towel around herself and skipped down the stairs to the living room, where she kept her notebook full of her goals, plans, and decisions. She turned to a fresh page and started designing a new life, open-ended, creative, expansive.

Ana worked quickly, using concepts rather than specifics. On one side of the page she wrote things such as: travel, meditate, meet others who are questioning conventions, creative projects, yoga, spirituality, sex, music. On the opposite page she only wrote three words: children, money, parents. In the past she thought of these things as dead ends to the life she wanted to live. Now she saw them as puzzles that needed solving. With this new approach, the insurmountable became possible!

She realised that she needed time alone to properly consider what had been revealed to her. Writing things down was an excellent start, but pen and paper alone were not enough. The small room she had lived in all her life was not real. She had now woken up to find herself in the middle of a field, with every direction open to her.

The people who had guarded that room, whose opinion she cared for, were made of straw. She had it all wrong. The constraints and limitations that she had lived by were brought on by the opinions of those who didn't matter at all. If Bill, who she had trusted blindly, could ditch her for his own benefit, then individual relationships didn't matter in the way she thought they did. She didn't think that Bill was unique or even a bad guy. It was she who had misjudged the world. She alone had built all the constraints. She had allowed him to matter and to influence the one life she had. She had fantasised that she was permanently bonded, while in reality it was a temporary pairing lasting only as long as their motivations were aligned.

"Wow," she exclaimed out loud. Then she started laughing. A big belly laugh, one that let out all the poison and the pain of her misplaced loyalty. It was all a misunderstanding. Her misunderstanding. He didn't ditch her. They just parted to pursue different lives. There was a legal, financial, and social contract for her and Bill to be together forever. She kept her side and he walked away from his. That's all there was to it. His life was better now and so was hers. Of course, her life could have been a lot worse, but that would have been her fault, and her gullibility. It was naïve to think that two fallible humans could guarantee each other eternal love and never cheat on each other.

Ana felt enlightened and empowered. She was the ruler of her life and her decisions were her own. She didn't owe anyone anything. Not even her kids. She had nursed them through their vulnerable childhood and had taught them what the world was all about. Soon they would move on as well.

Would she feel the same way about her kids leaving as she did about Bill? Obviously not. It's an expected parting. Not full of recriminations and drama like the breakup of her marriage. She had dedicated time, effort, money, and a good part of her life to another human being, who had simply moved on and started a life in which she was peripheral.

"Ah ha!" Her eyes lit up. "I owe nothing to nobody." Her life was her own to do with as she pleased. But what about mum and dad? They were getting old. Soon they would need her to take care of them. This stopped her in her tracks. Here was an obligation that she couldn't walk away from. Had she stumbled on to a problem? She owed them her life and years of care. They hadn't broken the contract. Could she?

She thought about her daughters. Did she expect them to take care of her? Not while she was strong and capable. But what if she became incapacitated? Would she expect them to incorporate her care into their lives? She tried to be as objective as possible. It all had to do with money, she decided. If her own resources or the government couldn't take care of her, then she would expect her kids to step in. Would they? That she didn't know, and in all truth, she didn't want to know. What if they didn't? Assuming she had the money, her plan was to live independently. Everyone wants that, don't they?

Ana realised that she had to carve out time for herself to process these new thoughts. The fashionable thing to do was to go on retreat somewhere. Closing her notebook, she opened a fresh page on google and typed: "change your life retreats." The paged filled with hundreds of options, almost all of them including a dose of yoga. She spotted India, Bali, Turkey, Spain, Costa Rica. She could literally go anywhere. Some of these retreats were outrageously expensive though.

She sorted the results based on price and discovered several that were well within her budget. Booking a retreat felt so indulgent that it made her head spin. Since she got married, their money had always been allocated to either the house or the kids. On occasion, they used their limited budget to upgrade Bill's car.

At the time she didn't really think of it as a sacrifice, but with her newfound clarity, she realised that it had been. Since her wedding day and especially once the kids came along, she worked hard for the future and to benefit the next generation. It occurred to her how preposterous this was. Each generation working hard for the next and no generation enjoying the present. Why do we do that? How has nobody noticed it before?

A sense of urgency overtook her. Before she had time to overthink it, she picked a beautiful retreat in a villa in Italy, and clicked, "BOOK." She filled out her credit card details and tapped her fingers while waiting for approval. Her heart was beating fast with excitement. There was no going back. The retreat was in two months. Her boss, Bill, and her kids would have to make arrangements around her and respect the time that she had booked for herself. She felt like saying, "fuck them," but decided that it was unnecessary. She substituted, "deal with it," instead. She emailed everyone her retreat dates and, satisfied, closed her laptop.

Chapter Twenty-Six

Ana gets married

When Ana realised the cost of getting married, she almost backed out. Bill, who had got out of getting a ring to save money, realised that the cost of a ring is a drop in the ocean compared to a full-blown wedding. Neither set of parents could afford to shoulder the cost, so it was left to the couple to decide how best to celebrate their union. Ana and Bill were in full agreement that they shouldn't bankrupt themselves for the sake of a party, and Ana's thriftiness confirmed to Bill that he had picked the right girl.

Ana was in her element. Staying within their meagre budget, she decided to put on a fabulous summer wedding. Her mum's wedding dress fit her perfectly with minimal alterations, and her favourite client volunteered their holiday home for the garden reception. Instead of hiring a photographer, they gave all the guests disposable cameras which they collected at the end of the evening. Ana enlisted her friends to handmake the wedding favours and table centrepieces. Even Thomas, her old flame, agreed to be the wedding driver in his flashy convertible, and he also brought a friend who was an amateur DJ. Their two dads coordinated an epic pig roast, and Ana assembled a giant wedding cake made from Waitrose cupcakes. Finally, Bill's dad loaned them the family campervan, which they took to Normandy for a romantic honeymoon. Everyone agreed it was a fantastic wedding and Bill beamed with pride as he kissed his newly wedded wife. They were a perfect match.

Chapter Twenty-Seven

Motherhood

After a year of setting up a home and getting used to married life, Bill asked Ana if she wanted to try for a baby. They calculated that it would take six months or so before she got pregnant, but to their surprise, a month after Ana stopped taking the pill, they conceived.

Even though her pregnancy was relatively easy, the reality of the massive life changes that lay ahead made Ana ambivalent about the future. She was never particularly keen on babies and children, but she hoped that once she could call them her own she would feel differently. So she took her daily pill of folic acid, laid off the wine and the sushi, and added ungainly loose clothing to her wardrobe.

Ana had no intention of leaving her career to become a stay-at-home mum. She made clear to her boss that she intended to work up to the last minute and that she would be back at work within six months. The week before her baby was due, her water broke during a client appointment. The client, a man in his sixties, had the presence of mind to put her in a taxi to the hospital, but not before Ana called maintenance to come and clean the mess. In the taxi she called Bill, who whooped all the way to the maternity ward.

Hannah arrived into this world red faced and angry. She screamed and screamed and refused any attempt to breastfeed her. This was fine with Ana, as she found the whole idea slightly distasteful. She had seen one of her co-workers, who had given birth a year ago, fiddle with breast pumps and wipe her leaky breasts, and she had no intention of repeating that experience.

Intellectually, Ana died when baby Hannah started to interrupt her regular sleep. Within a week of bringing her home, Ana moved to the guest bedroom so that the wailing, vampiric baby that never slept didn't disturb the slumber of the great provider. In fact, she proposed this herself in order to avoid Bill's morning moodiness.

"I have to get up at six every morning to get ready for work to feed this family. I can't be staying up all night," he told her. "You can nap during the day, go to lunch with your friends, go shopping and to the park. It's like a holiday for you. Please try to keep things quiet at night for me, okay?"

Ana didn't think it was like a holiday at all. She was exhausted all the time and the baby never stopped crying. Hannah slept during the day, but only if she was in motion, either in the car, or her pram, or in a sling on her mother's chest. This meant of course that Ana had to be awake to get Hannah to sleep. She was so tired that during those first few weeks she fantasized about handing over the baby to the first person who knocked on her door, and then collapsing in her bed for twenty-four hours of uninterrupted sleep. The grandparents from both sides of the family were elated about the new baby, but none of them offered more respite than a few hours of weekly visits, and of course when they came they needed entertaining themselves.

Things got better as time went by, and little by little, Ana found a balance in her life that allowed her to catch up on sleep, but she was not a natural. She did her motherly duties, and Hannah was always well fed and cared for. But she didn't like it. Above all, she resented her new life where the highlight of the day was pushing Hannah's pram up and down the supermarket aisles. Even this unsatisfactory outing needed at least an hour of preparation.

To break the routine, she often visited the baby groups recommended by her GP and even made a few new friends, but the topics of conversation were limited. Breastfeeding, baby pooping habits, and baby activities was all they talked about. What surprised Ana was that many of these women had impressive lives before having children. They had powerful jobs and were successful at what they did, but motherhood channelled all of their energy and competitiveness into the raising of their little prodigies. Which baby had gained the most weight and which mother had used the least pain relief during childbirth were hotly contested issues. Ana, who had a caesarean with full pain relief and did not breastfeed, quietly tolerated her diminished social status and wondered whether these ladies also refused pain relief at the dentists.

Six months went by, and Ana had to tell her boss that she would have to take six more months of maternity leave. The nursery fees for a baby under a year old were simply unaffordable. In fact, the nursery would cost more than her entire salary. To make matters worse, she found to her surprise that she would get no tax relief for the money paid to the nursery. She asked Bill whether he wanted to take some time off to care for Hannah while she went back to work, but he scoffed at the idea.

"Babies are a woman's job. Do you see any dads in the play groups? No, you don't. What would I do with Hannah all day?" Bill stopped to take a breath. "Also, I just got a promotion at work and I'm making more money that you would. It makes no sense for me to take time off!" Subject closed.

For her first birthday, Hannah got the MMR jab and was packed off to nursery. Getting her out the door in the morning made Ana late for work, but Bill washed his hands of any involvement. He made it clear to her, "if you want to go back to work, you will be responsible for dropping her off and picking her up. I can't leave a meeting or be late for work because of the baby. I hope you can see that." Ana couldn't really *see that*, but she rarely saw any dads at the nursery, so she didn't raise a fuss over it. She was just delighted to be away from the play groups and in the adult world again.

Soon she got into a routine that sort of worked. She would get up an hour before Bill, make breakfast, shower and get ready, wake up Hannah and get her ready, and while Bill ate breakfast and sipped his coffee, she would drop Hannah off at the nursery. She did most of the household admin during her lunch hour and the chores during the weekend, in which she cooked and froze all the dinners for the week to come.

At exactly 5:30 p.m. she had to leave work to pick up Hannah from the nursery. Often, she had to inform clients on the phone that she had to cut their conversation short to pick up her baby. Most clients were understanding, but a few complained to her manager. Ana received a warning, and for the first time in her career she was not considered for a promotion that should have been hers.

Her manager was clear. "For this job, I need someone who can stay late and is able to travel. I really like you Ana, but it would not work for you." Ana asked Bill whether he was willing to help with Hannah and pick her up occasionally when she had a meeting. He begrudgingly agreed. However, whenever Ana asked him to make good on his promise, he often found that he had a prior commitment, which always trumped Ana's.

Since the baby, sex had not been a priority in Ana's mind. She felt fat, unsexy and exhausted, and when she got into bed having sex was the last thing on her mind. Bill, who always got his full eight hours of sleep, had other ideas and within two years Ana was pregnant again. She called Meghan and burst into tears, feeling sorry for herself and wondering where in her busy day she would find the time to accommodate another baby. Before she even told Bill, she seriously considered having an abortion. But, of course, she didn't. "I don't want another baby," she confided to her sister Tracy, "at least not so soon. After having Hannah it somehow seems wrong to get rid of a baby. It feels like I know her already."

"How do you know it's a girl?" asked Tracy.

"Well, I don't know for sure, but I have a feeling that another girl is on the way."

Tracy never returned from her studies in Boston. The states had been great for her. She had met the man of her dreams and her job was full of promise. Away from their parents, who always treated her as the baby, she flourished. Ana suspected that Tracy stayed away to shake off the idea that she would be the caretaker of the family. Everyone knew that Ana was not fit for the role, but Tracy, with her mild manner and caring disposition, was always considered a likely candidate. In fact, Tracy surprised everyone by declaring that motherhood was not for her, and that she much preferred a life of hard work, love, and adventure. In the midst of her second pregnancy, Ana felt extremely envious and wished she had done the same.

Linda arrived seven months later to complete the family. This time Ana was prepared, and the experience was not as hard as it had been with Hannah. Linda was a much easier baby. She laid happily in her cot and gurgled at her sister. In the beginning, Hannah was ambivalent about the whole thing, but Ana let her play mummy and the excitement of having her own baby to feed and push around won her over.

Soon it became apparent that Ana would not be going back to work. The whole idea of dealing with a demanding job, taking care of two small children and running a household seemed overwhelming. After discussing it with Bill, they agreed that it would be best if Ana was a full-time mum, at least until the girls started primary school.

"I now get it why women give up on work," Ana told her mum, during one of their long telephone conversations. "I always thought that stay-at-home mums were lazy or incompetent, but now I see that it's the only sensible choice for most women."

Debby agreed wholeheartedly that the demands of motherhood took precedence over Ana's career. There was a small part of her, however, that grieved for her strong willed and ambitious daughter. She knew that the transition would be hard for Ana, who would be giving up her independence and her dreams, at least in the short term. But this describes quite a lot of women, doesn't it?

.

Chapter Twenty-Eight

An Italian retreat

When Ana landed in Pisa, she couldn't contain her excitement. She spent three hours furiously writing in her diary, making long lists of what she wanted to gain out of the retreat. She didn't know how it would work exactly, but she wanted this week in Italy to be the starting point of her new life. The girls had the number for the villa and her phone was turned off at the bottom of her suitcase. Social media and minute-to-minute consumption of the news had been her mental crutch for years, but this was something she was determined to change.

At the arrivals hall, she spotted a guy with his back turned to her, holding a sign with the name of the retreat, "Gran Burrone, Montepulciano." A few people had gathered around him clutching their carry-ons. Some carried rolled-up yoga mats and Ana wondered whether she should have brought one. The man turned around and she stopped dead in her tracks. All thoughts of yoga mats were forgotten as she stared into the most beautiful blue eyes she had ever seen. He will certainly make it hard to concentrate.

Ana greeted him warmly. "I'm Ana, and I am here to change my life," she blurted, feeling a bit self-conscious and a bit silly.

"Graham," he said, reaching out for her hand. "Our ride is outside. You're the last to arrive. Shall we get going?"

The villa was spectacular and surrounded by rows upon rows of vines. It used to be a winery. Graham, who had come to Italy ten years ago, found the run-down place and bought it for a pittance. He spent years fixing it up until it was ready to receive guests. He wasn't interested in the vineyard, so he gave it on a long-term lease to a local wine maker in return for an unlimited supply of wine for him and his guests.

Six girls and two guys, mostly British, had booked Graham's retreat for that sunny June week. Sitting around the pool and admiring the Tuscany countryside, Ana quickly established that most of the participants, like herself, had been forced to deal with a big life change and were looking for direction. Her natural instinct as a mother was to listen to everyone's problems and try to help with sensible advice, but she held back. She was there to help herself, so she let everyone talk while she sank into her diary and her private thoughts.

Ana did all the exercises to the letter, and her workbook was quickly filled with her thoughts about life, her children, her divorce, and her burning desires about the future. She found it easy to discuss her innermost fears and insecurities with this group of strangers, perhaps precisely because they were strangers. She carried no baggage here.

They saw her as she was, in the present, and they had no preconceptions to cloud their judgement. It was this clear view of herself that Ana found the most useful. Nobody held back out of superficial politeness, and Ana made big strides towards her goal. She opened up like a flower, and with Graham's expert guidance she saw new opportunities and life options.

She had never done much yoga before, but here, on the green lawn of the beautiful villa, she discovered the allure of stretching into poses she didn't think possible. Graham, who was also the yoga instructor, was very hands on. Ana shivered with anticipation every time she saw him heading her way to correct her posture.

At night, she dreamed about him, but not in a romantic, girly way. In her dreams he would creep into her room in the dead of night and lay next to her. Without speaking, he would pull down her panties and slide two fingers inside her, rubbing her, first gently and then hard. She would turn towards him as she felt him getting hard and would open up to him, begging him to enter her. As he slid inside her she would wake up, dripping with sweat. During those early mornings, as she lay in her bed hot with desire, she wondered what Graham would do if she slipped into his room unnoticed by the others. Would he fuck her?

Ana understood that vulnerable women often developed a crush on their spiritual leader, especially one as good looking as Graham, but this didn't stop her from wanting him. For sure, the other women did too, but during the retreat Graham remained detached and professional, and gave no sign that he wanted to reciprocate any advances. Glad that she had brought her vibrator along, Ana decided to concentrate on the reason she had come to Montepulciano.

By the end of the week, Ana had the beginnings of an exciting life plan and was charged with energy to get started. Her time away from work and the daily drudgery of caring for everyone had certainly given her the space to consider what she really wanted to do. The stillness of the yoga and the long hours of meditation had the effect of reminding her of the person she was, before marriage and motherhood turned her into unpaid help. She had been pretty awesome.

Ana wasn't sure she fully identified with this girl from the past, but she wanted to. Not just for herself, but also to show her daughters that their mother had a life before they came along. That she had been more than the person who cooked their meals, made sure they did their homework, and discarded by their father when he found a newer model. She wanted them to see the dangers that can befall a woman who forgets who she is and what she wants. She wanted them to understand that what happened to her could happen to any of them. She didn't want to teach them to hate men. Oh no. She wanted them to understand that marriage and family should involve give and take from both parties and that neither should sacrifice their identity at the altar of marriage.

During the retreat, her mistakes had been revealed to her thick and fast. By giving up on her career, allowing Bill to dictate the terms of surrender, and making the children her sole life goal, she had totally forgotten her agenda. She had wavered and then stalled, and her life had gone from an adventure to a white-collar prison. She hadn't progressed in twenty years, and this is why she chose to go right back to the same job she left in her thirties, doing the same things that she would have done if she hadn't met Bill. Graham had forced her to face her decisions.

She went over her notes and what she had written in her diary. What jumped out at her, clear as day, was that she needed her freedom, not just from people, but from her current life. She had always been a creative free spirit, yet she had lived most of her life anchored to a three-bedroom suburban home, most days going no further than Tesco or the school run. What a waste! Determined not to let her past get in the way, Ana returned to London full of plans and ideas. She didn't want to wait until it was the *right time* to make things happen. Come hell or high water, they would happen now!

Chapter Twenty-Nine

Serene suburbia

As their friends started having babies and getting married, they moved away from Shoreditch, and Bill started pressing Ana to make a similar move. "Honey, do you want our children to grow up in a flat on top of a nightclub? They should have a garden where they can play in the mud and discover nature, and we barely fit in this flat. Surely it's time to consider a house, maybe even a dog."

Ana, who saw Shoreditch as the last bastion of her real self, was resolute that she wouldn't become a desperate housewife in the suburbs. Bill was insistent, but it was Ana's flat, so he couldn't win this one as easily as some of the other battles he chose to fight. Finally, after a year of discussions, they reached a compromise. Ana would lease out her flat and continue paying down the mortgage from the rent. Together, they would buy a house in a suburb no further than thirty minutes from Central London by train.

On a rainy September morning, one that reflected Ana's mood, they loaded their household onto a moving van and waved goodbye to the doorman of the nightclub and the man at the local takeaway. The house they bought, after much searching and negotiations, was a three-bedroom semi-detached house with a good size garden. Even though Ana didn't relish the idea of Hannah and Linda rolling in the mud, she admitted that it was a far better environment for her daughters to grow up in, and the nearby schools were excellent.

The house needed lots of work, but her and Bill were both handy, and not afraid of hard work. They did most of the work themselves, only hiring help for specialised projects. The babies were content to crawl around their parents as they painted and moved furniture, and everyone was caught up in the excitement of the new home. Ana forgot her reservations, and soon made friends with the other mums in the neighbourhood. She felt settled and content. The girls were thriving, and Bill discovered that he had a talent for BBQs.

Compared to Shoreditch, life in the suburbs was easy. The supermarket was around the corner and had ample parking. There was parking everywhere, and she could get a doctor's appointment within a day.

In the years that followed, slowly and inexorably Ana morphed into a suburban housewife, indistinguishable from all the other women she encountered at the school gates. The primary topic of conversation was the children, followed by school events, kids' parties, home improvement and holidays. The only link to her old life was Bill, who commuted to the city everyday bringing back news of the markets and various rumours that were going around.

Occasionally he would bring a colleague home for dinner, but he mostly met co-workers and clients in the city after work. On those nights, Ana felt a little stab of regret that she had given up her career and that the only drink she ever had was a coffee with other mums at the local café, while the babies milled about and ate things of the floor. But then she reminded herself how lucky she was to have a beautiful home, two wonderful children, and a hard-working husband.

Bill leaves the house at seven in the morning and doesn't come home until seven in the evening, so Ana did all the childcare completely on her own. She didn't mind. She picked up new skills such as ironing, cooking and shopping for baby clothes on eBay. Ana's days were full, and she couldn't imagine how she had found the time to do all that *and* go to work while Hannah was a baby.

Ana had met many other mums in the park and in toddler groups and had formed friendships of convenience. They picked up each other's kids from school, had play dates, and visited restaurants, playgrounds, and sometimes galleries and museums, but Ana missed having adult conversations. Bill would come home from work shattered. For most of the evening he was in no mood for talking, and after taking off his suit he would turn on the TV and have a beer while Ana set the table for dinner.

Then she met a woman called Jane in a supermarket aisle. Both of them had prams and a toddler each. Jane's little girl of about four was pulling down all the colourful boxes from the shelves that she could reach, and Hannah was immediately attracted to the game. Jane was patiently stacking them back on the shelf while keeping a steady stream of chatter with her daughter. As Ana reached out to help, they smiled knowingly at each other like most mothers do over their toddler's heads.

"I think we have met before" ventured Ana.

"Yes, yes," agreed Jane. "We met at the baby music group last week."

The two of them hit it off right away and became inseparable. Unlike the other mums she had met, Jane was happy to venture far and wide with the babies, and together they would often travel up to London to go shopping and meet friends for lunch. Sometimes Meghan would join in, but not often. Her four children meant double the work for Ana and Jane, and that made it difficult. There was also something off about the relationship of her two friends that bothered her, but Ana couldn't put her finger on what it was.

On these outings, they sometimes talked about their husbands, but not often. The arrival of the babies had somehow reduced their importance in their lives. After all, both husbands were away for twelve hours a day, and all the common interests they used to have had evaporated. Beyond the basics, Ana exchanged few words with Bill during the work week.

She would ask about his day and he would mumble something back, still looking at his phone or the TV. He would ask about her day at the dinner table and Ana, desperate for an adult conversation, would launch into a stream of chatter that made him wish he had never asked. Most of what they said was directed to their children. On the weekends they almost always went their separate ways. Bill would take the kids to the park to give Ana a couple of hours to herself. She would go to yoga or simply have a long bath. Then it was her turn to watch the kids while he went to his Sunday football game and caught up with his friends at the pub.

Ana eventually had to admit that they had nothing interesting to say to each other. All their interactions involved family admin and were completely devoid of emotion, warmth or interest in each other's life. Whenever they went out to dinner with friends, they drank a lot, and mostly talked about the kids, their holidays and home improvements.

She often wondered if it was the same for all couples. It certainly was for Meghan. Her relationship with her husband mirrored Ana's. It suddenly made sense to her why stay-at-home mums had affairs or hooked up with their tennis coach—at least in the movies. They were terribly bored. She, of course, would never do such a thing. Even if she wanted to, she couldn't imagine where she would meet a man, or how she would find the time away from her daughters to have an affair. Also, to have an affair she needed a sex drive, and that had disappeared even before Linda was born. Bill's seemed to have disappeared as well.

The thought of sex only made her tired. As she lay next to Bill each night, she fervently wished that he wouldn't make a move, and her wish was granted. At the same time, she felt bad that he didn't seem to desire her at all. At the play groups, the women sometimes talked about their dwindling sex lives, but they made a joke out of it. In truth, Ana worried more about the lack of warmth than the actual sex. It bothered her that Bill never touched her or hugged her in public, or even in bed. Whenever she saw couples holding hands, she envied their relationship. What had happened to hers?

"Babies. That's what happened," Jane told her with authority as they strolled in the park. "Don't worry, of course he loves you. It's just a different kind of love, deeper and more meaningful. You are the mother of his children, you have built a life together. As the girls grow older and go to school things will change."

Chapter Thirty

The school years — desperate housewives

Ana held on to this thought as the years passed. When both Hannah and Linda had started school, Ana found that she had a little bit more time, but she convinced herself that it wasn't possible to go back to work. School finished at three, and then there was the shopping, cooking, and laundry to be done while the girls were doing their homework. She couldn't see how it was possible for her to drop the kids off at school and then make it to work by nine. Picking them up would be just as difficult.

The after-school club closed at six on the dot, it was expensive, and there were penalties if a parent was late. There were a few mothers who were managing it, but Ana was sure that they had help from grandparents or nannies. In truth, she was not sure, because these mums never lingered at the school gates or had time to chat. They would arrive in their suits and full makeup, quickly drop off their kids and then head to the train station. Ana wasn't even sure where they lived as they didn't mix socially with the non-working mums, not even on the weekends. Ana assumed they were too busy catching up with the housework that had piled up during the week.

To Ana, who had been out of work now for four years, they seemed exotic and slightly aloof. She felt pangs of jealousy when she compared their immaculately tailored suits with her greying tracksuit bottoms and hair that hadn't seen a hairdresser since Linda was born. Sometimes she would go home and start looking for jobs on the internet, determined to return to work sooner rather than later. Then the overflowing washing basket would catch her eye, or Jane or Meghan would pop over for a coffee, and the moment would pass.

"We should get back to work soon," she told Jane. "What are we going to do when the kids grow up and leave? It will be too late to go back then."

Jane laughed at the suggestions. "Ana you are not thinking straight! Have you seen those working mums at school? Do they look to you like they are having fun? They probably have to work. We don't. Enjoy this time with the girls. When they are grown up, we will have a brief time off, and then we will have grandchildren to take care of." The thought of taking care of grandchildren didn't cheer Ana up at all. It was a woman's lot to always be caring, caring, caring. Always caring for someone.

Ana rarely spent much time pondering philosophical issues, but Jane's comment got her thinking. Was it possible that her entire life's work would amount to this, living in suburbia with a guy who paid her no attention, while eagerly waiting for hypothetical grandchildren to dedicate her golden years to? Was she right to be aching for more? She thought of the other mums at the playgroup. They seemed happy, satisfied. Perhaps she should ask what they thought about their lives.

Jane seemed content being a mum. One afternoon in the park, over a bottle of pinot grigio, babies occupied chasing a squirrel, she opened up to her friend.

"I feel unfinished, unsatisfied," Ana confided, "like my life was on a rocket and then I was taken off and given a scooter, and then told that I could look forward to a wheelchair in the future, and that I should be happy with that!"

Jane looked at her friend thoughtfully. "Nobody knows what the future holds sweetie, all I'm saying is that this is a stage of life for us women and at this stage we have everything we need. Healthy children, hardworking husbands, beautiful homes and friends. To be complaining about that is ridiculous. What else would you want right now?"

Jane was right. She did have everything. Well, almost everything. Her sex life was dead but perhaps she could revive it, if she could be bothered.

Chapter Thirty-One

Ana revolts and finally makes things happen

Before the plane had even landed, Ana drafted her resignation letter to the bank. She would give them a month's notice. Then she had a thought. Perhaps she could get a year's sabbatical. Sally would certainly give her a good word if the alternative was to lose Ana for good. A year would be enough time to sort herself out. She felt quite proud of her breakthroughs. The two big obstacles to her spreading her wings had been her finances and caring for the girls. Now she had a solution to both.

She arrived home on a Saturday, and the next morning she started looking for estate agents. She decided that she would move back to her flat in Shoreditch. It was almost paid off and there was a direct train and a bus to the girls' school. She would take the small bedroom and the girls could share the main one. She composed an email to her tenants, giving them three months' notice to move out. They had lived in the flat for five years and she knew they would be devastated, but three months was sufficient to find another place, even in London.

When Hannah and Linda came back that evening from visiting their dad, she told them of her plan, and all hell broke loose. Both of them poopooed the plan and told their mum that they would not move under any circumstances or agree to share a room. Ana, who had foreseen their reaction, looked at her daughters coolly.

"I am afraid that you will have to move. I cannot afford this house any longer and I refuse to let it be a millstone around my neck. You are out of the house most of the day and the few hours you're here you just spend in the living room. You will have to adjust to our new circumstances."

Hannah, who would be leaving for uni in a year's time anyway, was the first to speak. "Why can't you wait a year until I'm gone? It would be so much easier!"

Linda agreed. "Then we won't have to share."

"I am done waiting!" Ana retorted. "I waited eighteen years to have a life. I have hated this suburb since the day your father insisted that we move here. Now I can decide where I'm going to live, and it will not be in an overpriced house in a boring suburb. I am sorry," she concluded, even though she wasn't a bit sorry.

She challenged her daughters to continue, but they wisely decided that it was the wrong moment to do so. When their mum was in this kind of mood, they would never win or make her change her mind. To demonstrate their displeasure, without a word, they went upstairs to their rooms. Later, when they came down for dinner, they presented their mother with a united front.

"Mum, if you force us to move to your small flat, we will go and live with our dad."

"You will do what?" She was incredulous. Ana felt like she had been stabbed. These children, that she had sacrificed everything for, were about to join the traitor over a shared bedroom? If she had any doubts about her strategy, this response made up her mind. Of course, she understood that her daughters were only using this as a threat, and that they had no real plans to move in with Bill and his new girlfriend, but it still hurt.

She took a big breath and faced the challenge head on. "You better give him a call and tell him then. I'm putting up the house for sale next week as soon as I pick an agent. I'm hoping to have it sold by the end of the summer, if not before."

Her daughters stared at her open-mouthed. They certainly hadn't expected this reaction from their mother. Their half-baked plan collapsed on the spot, and they started backpedalling. "Well we wouldn't go and live with dad full time, obviously. Just a few days during the week because it's close to school. He may not even have the space for the two of us to stay full time," said Hannah.

Ana knew that Bill's two-bedroom flat was only slightly bigger than her Shoreditch apartment. She was also sure that Bill wanted to enjoy his freedom with his new girlfriend and not be saddled with two teenage girls, no matter how much he loved his daughters. As upset as they had made her with their disloyalty, she didn't want them to feel unwanted or be rejected by their dad, so she relented.

"I'm sure he would love to have you stay with him, but I can't allow it. You will live with your mother, who has taken care of you all along. We will all move to Shoreditch together and I'm sure you will love it. It's full of young people, shops and cafes. Perfect for my two young ladies."

Their dignity intact, the girls held out an olive branch. "Can we have bunk beds? We always wanted bunk beds!"

Ana nodded enthusiastically. "The bedroom in Shoreditch is huge and has very tall ceilings. You can actually have a loft bed each with a wardrobe and a desk underneath. It will be amazing, I promise." With her small family in peaceful agreement, Ana served dinner and had her first glass of wine since the retreat.

The house was sold within a week of being listed, to a delighted family of four. As they strolled through the brightly painted kitchen that she had decorated herself, Ana was surprised that her only feeling was that of relief. She silently wished that this lovely family would make an acceptable offer so she could finally be rid of her suburban life once and for all, its lukewarm memories and its profound betrayal. The endless hours that she had spent lovingly and tastefully decorating the house paid off. The buyers made an offer on the spot. Her house was their dream home. It was all a matter of perspective it seemed. They could have this shell. Everything that it contained had turned to dust. Her future was elsewhere.

When Bill heard that Ana had sold the house and was planning to move to Shoreditch with the girls, he lost the plot. He was particularly upset when he found out that the house had sold for tens of thousands of pounds more than it had been valued during the divorce settlement. This, of course, wasn't Ana's fault. They had used a surveyor that Bill had chosen, and Ana agreed to.

In the weeks that followed, Ana received several emails from Bill. Some were matter of fact ("you will of course split the extra proceeds from the sale with me"), others were threatening ("you better respond, or I will take you to court") and a few were pleading ("I need the money to start my new life"). Ana was incredibly amused and didn't respond to any of them.

She had earned that house by sacrificing years of her life. The fact that the market was so positive was just her good luck. Bill finally wrote her a letter explaining how he had been extremely generous with the settlement, because he wanted his daughters to stay at the home they knew, and that she was a witch for moving them away from their childhood home. Ana, who had the memory of an elephant, clearly remembered the months following the separation and his ultimatums regarding the mortgage payments. She felt nothing but contempt for him and took great enjoyment in reading the letter to Meghan, while standing on the coffee table in the middle of the living room, that would soon be someone else's.

Ana completed on the house in August and had a big lawn sale, where everything that was redundant was sold to the highest bidder. She only kept a few things and got rid of everything else. It was a cleansing experience. Bill demanded that she send him the piano, which she was happy to do as nobody played it. In a final act of defiance, she also sent him the dining room table. She had bought that table without his approval, and because of that he never failed to say how much he hated it. Now he would have to fight his natural stinginess to get rid of it. She giggled at the thought of him eating on that table for the rest of his days, although she was sure he would probably try to sell it first.

Ana's tenants were not due to move out for another month, so she and her daughters were effectively homeless. With their stuff in storage and with the school term about to begin, both girls moved in temporarily with Bill. Ana examined her choices. Meghan graciously offered her guest bedroom, and of course her mum and dad also volunteered to put her up in her childhood bedroom, but Ana had other plans. This forced homelessness actually felt like a great excuse for an adventure.

After a bit of grumbling, Sally agreed to a six-month sabbatical, and even volunteered to give Ana half of any commissions that came from her clients. After paying off the small balance on her flat's mortgage, Ana felt comfortable enough to exchange her shit little car for a convertible. As she drove off from the dealer, with the top down, she made up her mind. She would go on a European road trip to find herself and decide what she wanted to do with the rest of her life.

Chapter Thirty-Two

Ana's diary

I went to collect the few personal belongings which...I held to be invaluable: my cat, my resolve to travel, and my solitude.

— Colette

It's the first day of my "discover yourself trip." Just drove for seven hours to arrive in the most beautiful location in France. As I turned from the highway into a very rural dirt road, the flat tyre indicator turned on. Hoping that it was an electronic fault rather than an actual flat tyre, I chose to ignore it. Centre Logan is a very quiet yoga and retreat centre, with a grassy camping site. It's just me and a little campervan with two German tourists, who appear to be asleep. They perked up when they heard me pulling up a few pitches to their left. I could see that they wanted company, but I'm happy on my own with my thoughts.

A Dutch guy, "Lucas," greeted me saying that he wasn't Dutch, he was human. The place is serene, and I'm alone with my little popup tent, a bottle of chilled sauvignon blanc and my laptop. Obviously, no WIFI. I'm not discovering anything yet, at least I don't think so. It's seven in the evening but still very hot. My camping stuff is still very disorganised, but I don't care. There is a stream running next to me. I wonder if it matters that I am getting old, or if it is a blessing. I'm not lonely. I feel totally at ease in my own company.

What will it feel like when I am too old to do trips like this one? Maybe it will be enough to do them in virtual reality when the time comes in twenty years or so. For now, I am capable and strong. But could this be an illusion. I'm wondering if my overwhelming need to start again is a sign that I don't appreciate what life wants to teach me.

A lot of people talk about stuff like that, but I think they're thinking of something different than me. I have no regrets. I see life as a game that I am halfway through playing. I would love to get into another other person's head and see what they're really thinking and what it means to them. Is there really a lesson in all this? Who is the recipient of such a lesson and why is it important? It's all so short anyway. I am full of experiences now, but why does it matter? What am I supposed to learn?

The older I get, the more I'm quite sure that we are here to live, and that's it. Everything else is stuff that people need to make them feel better about being on this earth. Human relations are mostly fragile and easily broken, despite promises. We depend on other people because this makes us feel like we are not alone, and someone is looking after us.

But it's an illusion. Relationships are fragile and people change. Bill changed and I didn't notice. I probably changed as well, but we kept going as if we were those same people that met each other twenty years ago.

It's very beautiful this morning. I slept many hours and woke up very early, with birds singing and the phone ringing. Somebody in a faraway call centre trying to sell me something at 5:30 in the morning. I was a little worried about the tyre and folding up the tent on my own. And I was totally right to be worried about the tyre. This morning it was as flat as a pancake.

Yesterday was a day of chaos chasing tyre dealers across France!

Finally, I was on the way with two new tyres. My next stop was a writing retreat in Italy. Quirky and welcoming, I absolutely love staying here. With literally hundreds of potted plants and blooming sunflowers, it's a place you never want to leave, unless the unbelievable heat drives you away. I slept in a magnificent bedroom in the cross-breeze of two fans, and I dreamt of sailing in a gale.

Travelling on my own and camping is a completely different experience to travelling with friends, children or a partner. I don't feel at all lonely or in need of company. I've been listening to my audiobooks, eating whenever I feel hungry, drinking wine, pitching my little tent, and loving every second of this trip. I really enjoy the camping aspect of it, and the funny looks I get from elderly couples when I rock up in my convertible and pitch my popup tent, before I pore my cold white wine and start writing on my laptop. I have been jokingly calling this trip my "self-discovery" adventure, but it's turning out to be that way. Don't ask me what I've discovered, it's too fuzzy…

I am now in Tuscany, near Florence, and there are vineyards and olive trees. The campsite has an infinity pool and totally finite connectivity. The internet only works if you perch at the reception booth. I bought a bottle of the local wine and jumped in the pool (without the wine).

I continued south. My next stop was Miturno, a family holiday spot with a string of campsites right on the beach. It looked a bit run down, but my spot was on the waterfront. It was grassy and I had my own large sink. Quite perfect really…except for the fire! As I was relaxing on the beach, I saw what I thought was a cloud. But then I smelled the smoke, which kept building behind the pine trees on the hill over the campsite. The smoke kept building, and then suddenly there was a whoosh and giant flames leaped over the trees. I didn't wait to see more. I ran to my tent and threw everything in the car.

Sparks were flying and a spot of yellow grass in front of my tent caught fire. I doused it with a bottle of Pellegrino, jumped in the car, and drove off. I didn't think I would ever see the tent again and wondered where I would find another charger. All around me people were running towards the exit and there were no fire engines in sight.

I drove about two kilometres away and sat in a little seafront cantina to wait it out. Soon, a helicopter started flying over, dousing the flames with sea water. I had visions of my half-burned tent covered in sea water as I scoffed down a plate of giant shrimp and drank a bottle of cold white wine. It turned out that my tent survived the fire, but not completely unscathed. There are little holes where the sparks have melted the fabric. No worries, I have better ventilation.

One of the things about this trip is that I can listen to my audio books undisturbed. I just finished an extremely intriguing book by Michael Pollen called *How to Change Your Mind*, that discusses experiments with psychedelic drugs and how by suppressing the ego they let you see the bigger picture. There is currently research being conducted around the world on this. I will look at it when I'm back because it suggests that this could be the route to experiencing death without dying. Intriguing.

I have to say that my mood has lightened quite a bit since the first day in France. I was never really unhappy, just not very hopeful about the future. We are quite delicate entities in that regard. There is something going on. I feel like I am in the middle of a million flying pages, and I can read what flies in front of my face. Slowly they are forming a book. A book of revelations and truth. Books, movies, conversations, music and even my own thoughts are saying the same thing, just a bit differently. Where is my mind?

Maybe I need to make a list of what matters and what doesn't and concentrate solely on what does. Kids, boyfriend, friends, true feelings, love. Dare I also add being thin? Surely I have an eating disorder.

I had a terrible night a few days ago. I discovered that one of the sparks had gone right through my tent and burnt a hole in my sleeping bag. I drifted off sniffing the acrid smell of smoke, a sure recipe for nightmares, which is exactly what I got. Dreams of my boyfriend running away from me as flames enveloped my tent made for a very disturbed sleep indeed. I was happy to see daylight and I packed my stuff quickly and got on the road as soon as I could.

Heading further south, I decided that I wanted to capture the feeling of awe from nature. I took a boat trip to the nearby island of Stromboli, which has a continuously erupting volcano. It was very cool to watch, but I didn't get the awe effect. I have seen lots of beautiful nature over the years, but the awe eludes me. Sometimes I wonder if I'm damaged, or if everyone else is deluding themselves or simply making it up. Maybe we are all lying to each other and the lying has propagated a fake reality.

I just read an Instagram post about how we all have a pre-determined destiny that is screaming to be fulfilled. What a crock of shit. I felt an intense desire to meet the author face to face and force him to admit the error of his ways. Nothing is pre-determined, thankfully, and everything that he thinks is supernatural is really only brain chemicals.

It worries me a little bit that I'm totally happy on my own and not missing anyone. Perhaps it hasn't been long enough. It's so great to only be responsible for myself and have space to dive into my own thoughts without being diverted or distracted. I wish I knew if I was unique or just honest. Is everybody thinking similar thoughts or do I stand alone?

On this trip, I feel like I'm growing mentally, extending what I thought was possible and understanding all the little

Anas inside me who have been trying to speak for years. I'm now listening and allowing them to surface. Since Bill left, I have been gradually uncovering more and more secrets about myself and my purpose on this earth. It is now coming together rapidly to form an alternate universe, where my existence is both more and less important. For the first time, I am seeing myself as a member of the universe rather than an individual at the centre of it. I haven't yet captured the idea that I am part of a whole, but I am beginning to understand it intellectually.

What can I do with this newfound knowledge and understanding? What does it mean and why should I care to have discovered it?

I had to cut my trip short and I'm now back in the UK, waiting for my biopsy results in a faceless hospital waiting room. I reached the south tip of Italy. While in the shower, I felt something that should not have been there. A lump on my right breast! I have always wondered what a lump would feel like and if it was easy to notice. Now that I have felt one, I can say with certainty that it can't be missed. It's a hard, irregular lump that doesn't give when pushed, on the upper part of my breast.

Feeling it was horrifying. Was I going to be the one in eight women that got breast cancer? Suddenly all my thoughts and writings about the meaning of life seemed like a bunch of nonsense. The ravings of a woman who had it all and was driving around Europe wondering about the meaning of life and whining about her little existential problems. Let me tell you, when death stares at you, like it is staring at me right now, the meaning of life becomes a minor secondary problem.

In the past week, I have regretted every cigarette and every glass of wine I have ever had. I have regretted painting my flat and inhaling the fumes. I have even regretted chewing the lead from my pencil when I was in primary school and eating red meat and salami. I have made ironclad promises to myself and god that if I survive this, I will live like a monk eating steamed vegetables doing yoga. I haven't told anyone, not the kids, not Meghan, not even my parents. I will wait and see what the doctor says.

The biopsy was a grim ordeal. Lying face down on a specially adapted bed, equipped with a hole for your breast to peak through, I felt totally exposed. My potentially diseased boob was forced through the hole and repeatedly stabbed with an instrument that took a sample of cells from the lump. Once this finished, I was sent home with a plaster and a leaflet to wait out the week. Of course, I didn't have a home yet, so I rented an Airbnb.

I didn't want anyone to know that I was back so soon or the reason why I had cut my trip short. But staying on your own in rented accommodation while waiting to find out if you're dying from cancer is not a good idea. During the week, I often broke down, and I almost called Meghan. The thought of dying brought home the true consequences of losing my life partner. I felt alone and I was terrified. Not of dying, but of dying slowly, painfully, and alone. I had my daughters, my parents, my sister and my friends, but despite that, it felt like I was in a room alone, and even though I could see them through the window, they couldn't touch me, and I couldn't get out.

I knew something was wrong when my name was called. A nurse guided me very tenderly into a softly lit private room and sat across from me while we waited for the consultant. A very young doctor—she must have just graduated—walked in, looking downcast.

"Mrs Sanderson," she said, without really looking at me. Looking at the wall behind me, she continued with what I already knew she was going to say. "I am afraid I have some bad news. The lump in your breast is cancer. I will refer you to an oncologist who will advise you on your options."

In life we feel like we have options. Often, they are limited or unpalatable, but they are almost always there. When you are told that you have stage three breast cancer, it feels like your options have disappeared. You either have treatment or you die.

Now I feel trapped. The walls are closing in and my choices have disappeared along with my previous ponderings about the meaning of life. I have much more urgent things to ponder, it seems. My cancer is aggressive and in a hurry to kill me. It skipped over stage one and stage two and went straight to my lymph nodes. My tumour is larger than a grapefruit, and small clusters of cancerous cells are in three of the lymph nodes. The consultant made it clear that the only treatment option I have is chemo, and lots of it, followed by surgery to remove the tumour.

As soon as I got home, I googled stage three, grade three breast cancer survival rate. Statistically, seventy-two percent survive for five years. These are good odds, but it doesn't change my mood. The fragility of life has been revealed to me in a pretty shocking way and at the worst possible time, in the middle of a move, with two teenage daughters going through exams. Pretty shit.

I only told Meghan. A week after my diagnosis, she was helping me move into the flat. My composure crumbled. She found me sobbing in the kitchen over a broken teacup. I wouldn't stop, I couldn't stop.

"I have cancer," I blurted out between rivers of tears. "I am so afraid." In truth, the favourable statistics have reduced my fear, but losing my hair is an unbearable prospect. I have a funny shaped head that is flat at the back, and I know I'll look terrible. And what a way to begin my life in trendy Shoreditch!

Ever since, Meghan has been amazing. She came with me to every chemo appointment, cooked for the girls, found a wig maker and held a bucket for me when my nausea got too much. Together we had a long chat with the girls to reassure them that I wasn't dying. In the beginning, they were weepy and solicitous but within a few weeks they returned to normal.

I feel that I was given too much hope that I wouldn't lose my hair. They put a cold cap on my head during treatment, which sometimes helps. Google also informed me that thirty-five percent of women don't lose their hair. Three weeks after my appointment I almost clogged the drain when I was taking a shower. The statistics were against me. To be honest, I briefly considered skipping chemo altogether, just because I didn't want to lose my hair. I found plenty of evidence online about women who cured their cancer by eating seeds and other natural remedies.

The foolish idea that I still had options was extremely appealing, but Meghan forced me to confront the fact that I had none. I had two daughters to care for and the conventional way was the only way if I wanted to continue occupying the mortal world. I did have a little bit of control over my fate. As soon as I realised that I was part of the sixty-five percent who would lose their hair, I pre-empted the slow shedding and had it all shaved off.

With my hair gone, I had officially become a cancer sufferer, and the suffering began. Of course, I ignored it as much as possible, and on good days I went to the gym, but I was nauseous, cold and bald. My pre-cancer life feels quite idyllic by comparison, but without cancer I wouldn't have known that.

Everywhere I go these days I get looks of pity. That is when people even dare to look at me. Often, they avert their gaze when they catch mine and pretend to look at their feet or at something past me in the distance. I'm seen like an alien by those around me and I feel like I occupy a different universe. When they're forced to speak to me, I detect a tone of reverence and respect, a tone that people reserve for the terminally ill and the dying. Sometimes they tell me stories of cancer survival and propose "remedies." Other times they scare me with their stories. I think it's because they are afraid themselves.

Nobody, not even Meghan, treats me like they did before the cancer. My friends don't recognise me, and this is the second cut, the one that cuts the deepest. I am still

Ana, but somehow nobody can see it. All they see is the cancer. This is the problem with cancer. Your disease is out in the open and can't be kept confidential. You can't suffer in silence, unless you stay indoors and see no one.

Despite the hair and the nausea, I decided to go back to work. I needed the money and being at the office makes me feel normal. I can't decide if Sally was happy to hear that I would be coming back. She's afraid that clients will shun me because of my bald head. I agree with her, so I bought a very expensive and professional looking wig for my client meetings.

I would have liked to be able to wear it all the time, but it's incredibly hot and uncomfortable, and it sometimes slides back and gives me the forehead of a giant! In the privacy of the office I wear scarves. Scarves make those around me uncomfortable, which is a funny thing. They all know that I'm bald, but when I wear a wig, they treat me almost normally. When I wear a scarf, they treat me like I'm sick.

Sally told me that I can work from home as often as I like, "so that I don't have to tire myself with the commute." But I know that the reality is that she doesn't want to have to deal with me and my bald head. This of course defeats the purpose of being at the office and feeling normal, but often I don't feel well enough to go so I've taken advantage of the offer on more than one occasion. Clients haven't noticed that anything is amiss. I always wear my wig for those meetings, and clever makeup covers the missing eyebrows and eyelashes.

When I'm at work, I'm not as scared. The office is respite from the idea that I, too, can die. That my body has staged a revolution and the breasts that have fed my daughters and signalled my womanhood are trying to kill me.

During the day, I go to the ladies' room to obsessively check that my wig is sitting right. I feel an incredible shame when it comes to my baldness. I admire those women who are able to walk with their bald head held high in broad daylight. I'm trying to examine why my cancer and my baldness are a source of shame. I didn't cause it. I'm not responsible. Unlike my divorce, where I do feel a certain level of responsibility, this new calamity is entirely undeserved. I eat right, I don't smoke, I barely drink. It's just the luck of the draw. No reason to feel shame. Yet I do.

I feel singled out, marked, diseased, shameful, afraid, and undesirable, unwomanly, and ugly. It's all so clear to me now that I used to have it all and that the divorce was a minor inconvenience, or perhaps a stepping stone to much better things.

They say that the devil laughs when you make plans, and he (or perhaps it is a she) was certainly cracking up when he met me a few months ago, full of hope and promise. Perhaps god heard me wondering about the purpose of life and decided to give me a quick, hands-on lesson. In his infinite wisdom he probably thought that I would appreciate his crystal-clear message about how little I, Ana, matter in the grand scheme of things. Like everything else on this earth, I too will go. Now this lesson is more than just words in a book or some kind of philosophical diatribe. It is the tumour in my own body, the nausea and the handfuls of hair in my shower drain. Crystal clear, indeed.

What do people do with lessons such as mine? Is there something I should be doing, like appreciating every moment I have with those I love? Perhaps I should make a bucket list. But wait a minute, nobody said that I'm dying yet!

Chapter Thirty-Three

Bill, now

Bill was remarkably absent during Ana's cancer. He had shown no signs that he had even heard that the mother of his children, who had shared his bed and cooked his meals for twenty years, was fighting for her life. In fact, he had heard, and he was worried. Not about Ana, oh no. He was worried about himself. As a fully-fledged hypochondriac, Ana's cancer felt like a threat. It was too close to home. If she can get it, he could get it too. He stayed away, as if her unfortunate luck was contagious. Ana knew him well enough to know that.

When it came to any mention of death and disease, Bill always froze with fear. He would obsessively research even the most minor symptoms and was on first-name terms with the family GP. Ana had a good laugh with Meghan imagining Bill in the office loos with his white shirt unbuttoned, checking his breasts for potential tumours.

But knowing why Bill had stayed well clear of her drama didn't make it any easier. Knowing that the person who had been with her for more than half of her adult life didn't want to see her during her most severe life crisis put a dent in her faith in humanity.

Not that her faith had been that strong to begin with. She had always been suspicious about even the purest of motives, and dismissive of grand gestures and promises of eternal friendship. But when it came to Bill, she had been fooled that he was different, that he was her soulmate, one of her tribe. Now her tribe was quite small: her daughters, Meghan, her sister and her parents. She had kept the full extent of her cancer from her parents. They were too far away to help and too frail to be told that their daughter may leave this earth before they do. Her two confidants were her sister Tracy, who was a whole continent away in New York, and of course Meghan, whose unwavering support she would never forget.

She tried to be honest with herself. Why did it matter that Bill hadn't acknowledged her sickness or offered any support? Did she still love him? No, she didn't. In fact, she felt a bit of disgust at the thought of his thin, pursed lips, short hairy legs and hunched shoulders. She had no love for him.

What would she do if he got cancer? She pondered the question and felt slightly embarrassed by the immediate flash of satisfaction she felt at the possibility that he would have to face the same fear that she was currently living with. If Ana would be exactly the same as Bill, maybe she shouldn't be so hard on him. Maybe she would be even worse, like pretend to care so that she could be close and watch him suffer. She smiled at her secret, devious thought and wondered if everybody else was like her, even though they would never admit it. Friends and family would remind her of the devastation that such an illness would bring to Hannah and Linda, and they would be right. But did this make one iota of difference to her inner satisfaction at Bill getting his just punishment? Nope, it did not. She was human, not evil.

Hannah and Linda, who didn't know about their dad's extreme fear of death and disease, were truly puzzled by his attitude. Ana considered it to be a blessing in disguise. Seeing their dad so unconcerned decreased their worry and anxiety, something Ana didn't want to have to deal with. Her mantra to her daughters was unwavering: "You don't need to worry about me. I am as strong as a horse. Nothing can kill your mother!" And they would feel much better, even if they were slightly unconvinced by her pale face and hairless scalp.

Ana worried about her daughters much more than she let on. If the worst happened to her, what would become of them? There was Bill, but he wasn't very proactive, and he was totally clueless when it came to his daughters and their growing pains. She knew that they would be lost without her and this thought occupied a good part of her waking hours. This, and of course, death.

Chapter Thirty-Four

The grim reaper

"Death. Why is it so scary?" Ana tried to put her thoughts on paper. It was a technique she had learned many years ago, which put things in perspective. She wrote:

Physical pain
Not being able to breathe
Seeing myself in the mirror and not recognising myself
The pain it will cause to those I love
The fear of non-existence
My body rotting
Being underground in a coffin

Her pencil hovered over this last one. Somehow, she couldn't imagine her body rotting. Her eyes falling inwards and disappearing, worms coming out of her cheeks. She shuddered at the thought of this face, this body that she had occupied for more than a half a century ending up like piece of meat that had rolled out of the shopping bag. She would smell. Her rational brain told her that this didn't matter. She would be dead. But of course, it did. Her body was her tenuous hold to life and the world that she knew. If it rotted away, where would she be? What would she be?

Raised in a household were god had no place, she now wished she was able to have faith. She wanted to believe in god and the afterlife, but her dad had done a number on her. His complete dismissal of the stories in the Bible, that he referred to as fairy tales and half-truths, had sunk in deeply, and Ana knew she would never be able to blindly believe in god. When she died, it would be the end of her. She wouldn't exist. Yet, Ana could not in any way contemplate a world that would go on without her. The thought of being obliterated made her panic. She wondered why that was. The inevitable ending is well documented and known to all from the very beginning.

Ana had read books that waxed lyrical about how all there is, is love. Books written by gurus who had meditated on the thought that we are all part of the universe and should therefore not be afraid of physical death. These teachings sounded comforting and idyllic when she first came across them but faced with the very real possibility of actually dying, she realised that she lacked that level of enlightenment. The spiritual and scientific wisdom, that she was energy and energy did not disappear, left her cold and uninspired. Becoming part of the collective consciousness and discovering her higher self in the process also rang hollow. Did whoever wrote this nonsense ever face their own demise?

Perhaps she was being harsh, judging things she did not understand. She closed her eyes and chanted. "I may be dying, but my higher self will merge into the collective consciousness, and thus, I will never cease to exist." She stopped. Did she buy this? She didn't really know.

Ana was haunted by regrets about people not loved, places not seen, experiences not tasted. It could all be over, and something inside her was screaming, "no, not yet! I am not ready. I have not lived." The years had flown by as Ana waited for the time to live, and as potential death approached her, she was gripped by a terrible fear of things that had been left undone or unfinished.

To ease her thoughts, she tackled her list methodically. She knew that physical pain could be completely eliminated with the right medicines. If it came to that, she would accept everything that was offered. She wanted to leave this world in complete unconsciousness and didn't understand the need of some people to stay *with it* as long as possible. This would take care of her fear of not being able to breathe. She crossed it off her list. She also drew a line through the next one. Withering away was scary, but only if you could see yourself. If all the mirrors were taken away, there would be no way to terrify yourself with your reflection.

The pain her death would cause others. Was she really afraid of that? No, she wasn't. She cared about her daughters of course, but not enough to keep it on the list. She was feeling much better already. It all came down to one thing: dying painlessly. This was fully within her control. She closed her notebook, turned off the light, and slept like a baby.

Chapter Thirty-Five

Life goes on

I am who I am
I am not who I would like to be
I am not who I should be
I am not who my mother would like me to be
I am not even who I used to be
I am who I am

— Jorge Bucay

As it turned out, Ana needn't have worried. Death didn't end up knocking at the door of her Shoreditch flat. She was one of the lucky ones. Ana knew that there was a chance that cancer would come knocking back, but for now she had a clean bill of health, and a full head of hair. It was only the small scar from her chemo port which reminded her of the darkness that almost overcame her a few months back.

In the weeks and months that followed the all-clear, she was in a permanent state of bliss. Everything made her happy and nothing bothered her. The girls with their petty squabbles, Bill's treachery and new life, Sally's vacuous behaviour while she was sick, the bus driver who would pull away from the stop without waiting. None of these previously infuriating situations could touch her now. They were still part of her universe, but she saw them differently. She understood that their behaviour was not in response to what she did, but in response to what they carried around inside them. She looked at the clenched jaw of the bus driver. She had gained the ability to see that he had nothing against her. Something external to her had made him angry, sad and frustrated. For that, she felt sorry for him.

Ana set out to make yet more changes, but this time she wanted drastic and meaningful changes. One thing she was sure about was that her days at the bank were numbered. She wanted to find another way to earn money in a job that she actually liked. Ana scoffed at her childish desire to discover herself while drinking wine in Tuscany. She dismissed the idea that a life of eternal adventure was what was needed to make her complete. Like everything else, the excitement would wear off and she would be back to where she started, only older and just as empty and clueless.

There was nothing to discover, only something to uncover. She had to peel away the layers of pretence that life had wrapped her in. Before the cancer, she thought that she knew everything about herself, when in fact she had only uncovered the first layer. In a race to beat time she had been trying to recapture the Ana of her early twenties, but she realised that this person was long gone. Trying to be that person wasn't a return to authenticity. She had been trying to live in a skin that she had outgrown. Ana was excited by this revelation, but when she talked to Meghan about it, she laughed.

"So, you have matured…It happens to all of us and often we try to find refuge in our younger selves. It's normal."

"But I want to grow as person, find wisdom, enlightenment, purpose." She stopped herself when she realised her mistake. She had been looking for growth by rejecting her past, instead of acknowledging that it was an integral part of who she was. There was no going back. Only forward.

If there is one thing that Ana discovered during her cancer, it was that she only had one friend, Meghan. Her circle—if you could even call it that—was really more of a square, consisting of her daughters, her sister, her parents and Meghan. This was pitifully small for someone who had spent more than half a century on this earth. Being honest with herself, Ana admitted that it was entirely her fault.

She had marched through life alone, judging everyone else to be an impediment to the way and the speed that she wanted things done. She thrived on judgment. She judged everyone all the time whether she knew them or not. She judged her daughters, Bill, and Meghan. But above all and perhaps more harshly than the rest, she judged herself. She began to realise how isolated this had made her. She never really gave people a chance to penetrate her shell to really find out who she was. And she never bothered to see the world through their eyes.

It occurred to her that she had been going through life at breakneck speed, as if the destination was a desirable place to reach. Everything and everyone that stood in her way was an obstacle to crush, and in that instant, realising that, she began to forgive Bill. She caught a glimpse of what his life had been like married to someone like her. She judged him, and he always came short. No wonder their sex life had gone to shit. She had made him feel less of a man, even though on the surface it was her who was submitting to his demands. She should have never been with someone like him. Her choice of this man had been her mistake. His current girlfriend, a pretty girl with a low-level job and minimum ambition was so much better suited to this average underachiever that she had married.

All was slowly being revealed and she was amazed at her previous blindness. All she had seen was her point of view, trapped in the suburbs, living a quiet life, while in reality she was an exotic bird that needed the Amazon rainforest. Meanwhile, Bill, a grey and unassuming pigeon, had been trapped in a room with a very unhappy exotic bird who had been pooping in his dinner out of sheer frustration.

In the early days of their marriage, he tried to keep up while hiding his fear of her, and what she wanted him to be and do. She wore a housecoat over her colourful plumage so that she could fit into his world. Her marriage had been a charade doomed to failure. How it ended was nobody's fault, and it was a very good thing. She felt a wave of gratitude towards Bill. His one and only show of courage had saved them both.

Ana felt light as a feather. How could she have been so blind, so clueless about her own marriage, her husband, her daughters and quite possibly the whole of the human race? She had always prided herself on her razor-sharp intellect and understanding of people and their motives, but she had totally missed the point. In seeing everyone as damaged she had judged them. If she saw them as different, she could love them.

All this was about to change. Ana started preparing for her life as an integral part of the human race. Her next goal was to form connections and give the people around her a chance.

Chapter Thirty-Six

A chance meeting with a real shaman

I love my past. I love my present. I'm not ashamed of what I've had, and I'm not sad because I have it no longer.

— Colette, Chéri (1920)

Ana loved the idea of a festival. When her downstairs neighbours Terry and James suggested an intimate music festival deep in the countryside she did not hesitate. "I'm in, and I'll bring the girls too."

Hannah and Linda, who had been raised like princesses, agreed to go, but only on the condition that there would be flushing toilets and comfy beds. Neither of these things were possible, so the girls bailed out. Surprisingly, Meghan jumped at the chance to come along and the two of them set out for a long weekend of fun.

At the festival campsite, they were greeted with cheers by a much larger group of campers than Ana had anticipated. There were seven large tents and two tipis, arranged in a circle with a gazebo in the middle. The tipis were magical with their oriental carpets, fairy lights and large, soft floor cushions. Several unusual instruments were carefully arranged around the perimeter of the larger tipi with a large drum dominating the centre.

It took Ana and Meghan ten minutes to set up their popup tent, mats and sleeping bags before they emerged in the sunshine to join the group. They were handed drinks, which they gratefully accepted, and also offered little blue pills, which they both declined. Even though they didn't know anyone other than Terry and James they instantly felt welcome, but also a bit intimidated by the eclectic mix of people. They were introduced to circus performers, musicians, nuclear physicists and extremely beautiful men and women wearing amazing costumes.

Ana and Meghan had packed a few things from their kids' Halloween selection, but they felt too embarrassed to wear them now they saw what the others had brought. Sensing their awkwardness, Terry ducked into his tent and reappeared with a large trunk which he set in front of them.

"You two are a bit underdressed, I'd say. Here is the communal wardrobe, pick out anything you like!" With a flourish, he opened the lid, and colourful feathers, hats and beads spilled out.

Suitably outfitted, Ana felt like she had been reborn into a magical woodland creature, who was allowed to engage in all sorts of weird and wonderful transgressions. After the third martini, they both agreed to give the little blue pills a go. Why not? Who the fuck cares about being proper? They were in the middle of a hippy commune that had welcomed them for a weekend of fun! Meghan agreed without much fuss, which surprised Ana.

"I always wanted to try ecstasy," she confided to her friend. "I just never thought I would get the chance." Swearing each other to secrecy, they swallowed their pills and the fun began.

Deep into the night, first around the campfire and later laying on the cushions in the tipi, they talked about life, love, friendship, and spirits. Everything flowed like it had always meant to. Ana felt love like she had never experienced before. Love for Meghan, her stroppy daughters, but also for these people she had only met today. It was an interesting experience, that opened a little window in her mind and showed her a different world. One that changed based on the angle that she chose to view it from.

Everything slowed and then stopped. She didn't have to go anywhere or do anything. She found herself routed to the present moment with a sense of calmness and relief. For someone like Ana, who had been on the go mentally and physically at all times from the moment she was born, this feeling was completely novel and wonderful. Unfortunately, it was also fleeting. She drifted off to sleep in full costume on the colourful cushions, holding her friend's hand.

The next morning, she woke up incredibly thirsty, but with a clear head. There were people around her still awake and still talking. Someone passed her a cup of coffee and a bottle of water. Meghan had left during the night and was still snoring in their little tent. Next to Meghan was one of the guys from the night before. He didn't look any older than twenty-five. Their heads were touching, and it was obvious that they were both naked under the sleeping bag that barely covered them. Ana tiptoed away, a bit shocked, but also slightly envious that her friend's night had finished with such swagger. Way to go Meg. She vowed to look out for opportunities herself.

Ana was beginning to believe that drugs were the answer to a better and more meaningful existence. She looked around the mingling group to see if any more of the blue pills were around, but instead she was offered a plate of fried eggs and a bit of toast.

"Today, we're hosting a drumming session with Mudang," she was informed by the girls sitting next to her. Under her face painting she looked to be about twelve, but Ana was sure they must be older. She thought that the drumming sounded boring. Finishing her eggs, she joined the long queue for the showers.

Ana needn't have worried that she would be bored. When she lay on the cushions in the tipi as part of the Shaman's circle, with a slightly embarrassed Meghan by her side, she had no idea that what was about to happen would profoundly transform her life.

Mudang was a very skinny man of indeterminable age, who also looked slightly dirty. He wore ill-fitting clothes of earthy tones. He was unimpressive and unassuming, and Ana wondered whether she should sneak out to join the lively group that was waiting for a gig. She looked around and saw that it wasn't possible, so she closed her eyes as instructed and listened to Mudang as he opened the session with a chant. Here we go.

"Perhaps we can catch up on our sleep," she whispered to Meghan, who looked the worse for wear. Mudang wanted to know if anyone was under the influence of drugs or alcohol. A couple of people got up and quietly left. Ana decided to stay. Mudang told them that the purpose of the gathering was to experience a journey where they would descend to another world and meet their spirit animals, who would guide them in the journey and give them instructions about the future. Ana perked up. She certainly wanted instructions about the future, but she wasn't really expecting anything to have an effect on her. She was simply too grounded in reality to allow spirit animals to appear, but if they did it would be fun.

The drumming started quietly and rhythmically but steadily gathered pace and volume. Soon it drowned out all other sounds and, surprising herself, Ana started falling into a trance. The blackness behind her eyelids was gradually replaced with colourful swirls and shooting stars. Ana felt sure that it was a delayed result of last night's ecstasy, but whatever it was, she was liking it.

She opened one eye and the colours disappeared. She caught a glimpse of Mudang. He had been transformed into a shaman for sure. His hair wildly swung in front of his glazed eyes while he banged on the ancient drum in front of him with an intensity that was not meant to be seen. Ana felt guilty and closed her eyes quickly. The swirls returned and the experience intensified. She was trying hard to see if the shape of an animal or plant had emerged to guide her as the shaman had promised.

The drumming had extinguished all her other thoughts and she was well and truly in the present. That alone felt amazing, but the spirit guide was proving elusive. Ana concentrated on the flashing lights behind her eyelids, until finally a shape began to appear. It never achieved full resolution, but Ana could clearly make out some big cat. A leopard? Perhaps even a lion. It never approached her or said anything to her. It just stood there in the distance, not coming any closer but not turning away either.

Ana, who was quite suspicious of all things supernatural and spiritual, got the message. Her spirit animal couldn't really guide her, because she hadn't decided, even at an unconscious level, where to go next. She stood at a crossroads, and her spirit animal stood there too. She felt love and sorrow at the same time for the big and lonely cat. It was her alright. It was an Ana that had not been tainted by painful experiences and disloyal people. A pure part of her that was waiting at the crossroads to guide her to healing and salvation. She was crying.

Then she was roaring. The big cat—a lioness—started walking towards her until it stood right next to her. She felt proud and strong, but above all she felt whole. Nothing was missing. All of her was there. Would she be able to bring the lioness back with her? As she savoured her wholeness, she begged for the drumming to go on forever. She roared again and her lioness roared with her at the same time. Then the drumming slowed down, and stopped.

As the drumming stopped, the festival noises invaded the tent. When she opened her eyes, she found herself in a world that was lacking and incomplete. The wholeness of the world had fractured. The shaman was dripping with sweat and Meghan, with her eyes still closed, was quietly sobbing. Others in the circle were quickly writing down the messages they had received from their guides. She didn't need to write anything down. Her message had been clear. She needed to become whole again and rise above the pettiness and anger that had consumed her thoughts. Her anger, fear and disappointment with how her life had turned out had wounded her and silenced her roar. Her spirit guide had shown her that nothing was lost, just misplaced, and still within reach.

Chapter Thirty-Seven

The festival fallout

Following the festival, Ana received a garbled message from Meghan. When she called back, she spoke to a woman who appeared to have lost her marbles. Meghan had done a runner with the guy from the festival, who was half her age and lived in a caravan in Cornwall, near St. Ives. Meghan rambled on about happiness, shamans, and how her spirit animal had guided her into the arms of her true love. From now on she was going to be called Sky and she would live in nature, weaving grass baskets to sell at the local market.

Ana's immediate reaction was to try to knock some sense into her friend, and then she realised that she wasn't going to. Meghan had found the courage to literally break every chain that keeps women shackled to their mundane reality. While men can gain their freedom by throwing a maintenance payment to their past lives, women can't. It is inconceivable to society and to the women themselves that they would run away from their responsibilities, simply because they had found a better option. When a husband leaves, he packs a suitcase and goes to a hotel, or moves in with his new lover. When a wife divorces, she keeps her old life, trying to shoehorn anything new into her stale reality. Meghan had turned her back on this model. She was the man! Ana loved her for it.

Before Meghan's news had a chance to sink in, Bill came knocking at her door, having realised that his new shiny toy was just that, a toy. He was bored of her. He missed his old organised life and impeccable home. He told an astonished Ana that she was the love of his life and that he had made a terrible mistake. Nothing in his demeanour indicated that he had any doubt that she would have him back. Ana was speechless at his audacity, but Bill took it as a sign that she was moved by his repentance. He walked past her, put his suitcase on the floor, and collapsed on the sofa.

"I remember this place," he said as he scanned the room. "Great little flat, but it will not work for the four of us. On the way here I had a look at what's on the market around our neighbourhood. We should probably get something smaller now that Hannah is about to go to uni, and we will need to rebuild our savings. Our breakup really took us way back financially."

Ana still hadn't found her voice, but inside she was screaming with indignation. Our breakup? *Our* breakup? Did he really believe that they were both responsible? Had he forgotten that he had walked out on them, left them penniless, and was totally absent during her illness? What is this love he talked about?

"You self-serving, intolerable bastard. How dare you show your face in my home! I would rather cohabit with a diseased toad, a whole family of diseased toads than you."

He looked at her uncomprehendingly. "But I came back, I love you, everything will be the way it was before. I've learned my lesson. Don't make this difficult for me," he trailed off. Something in her eyes should have signalled to him that it was dangerous for him to continue, yet he pressed on. "Don't be unreasonable sweet pea. Think of our children." She was incredulous. Now it was her fault. And by keeping his cool he was making her the irrational one. "I thought about you throughout your treatment. I just couldn't be with you. It would have been too stressful for me to see you sick and losing your hair. It looks nice this short haircut, but I prefer your hair a little longer."

Ana stood in front of him. "Bill, I could have a discussion with you about our marriage and *our* breakup. I could try to explain to you how I felt when you left me for another woman and didn't see me when I was sick. I could spend hours trying to convince you that you behaved in a wicked, shameful and unforgivable way towards me. But instead, I will just ask you to leave, now, right now and forever."

"But what am I supposed to do now, where do I go?" he whimpered, losing his bravado.

Ana, who had waited all her life for an opportunity to be Scarlet from *Gone With The Wind*, couldn't pass up the opportunity. "Frankly, my dear, I don't give a damn," she said, as she ushered him out of her house and her life.

The next person to come knocking at her door was not at all unexpected. Meghan's husband, Jim, dishevelled and looking lost, collapsed exactly where Bill had sat. Dark circles under his eyes told the story of his sleepless, tortured nights. Even though Ana fully sympathised with his plight, she remained loyal to her friend. Admittedly, she did feel a little guilty, having been the one who suggested going to the fated festival, but not guilty enough to take his side.

"What am I supposed to do without her? She is the best thing that's ever happened to me. She took care of everything."

Ana was sure she did. She recalled her friend lamenting that he never helped around the house.

"The kids are asking for their mother," Jim whined. Ana doubted this last statement. Meghan's four kids were grown up and only one of the girls was still at home, living quite independently and probably taking care of Jim as well.

"Give her some time Jim," she advised. "I think she needed some time to herself. She's been taking care of you and your four children and she never really had the time to go after her own goals."

Jim looked up at her sternly. "Ana, you and I know that her goal has always been her family. Besides, she's never worked a day in her life."

This statement was wrong on so many fronts that Ana didn't know where to start. "Jim, a woman that raises four children and takes care of a six-bedroom house with a large garden has more than a full-time job, and it's unpaid. Perhaps she feels that with the kids at uni she's allowed a vacation."

Jim was beside himself. "A vacation? What sort of vacation is this, running away with a man half her age to live in a caravan?"

Ana tried to suppress a smile. When Bill had left her for a younger woman, Jim had been quick to pontificate over a cold beer that sometimes relationships don't work out and a man has the right to seek his happiness elsewhere. Now the shoe was on the other foot. Why was it alright for a guy to leave his family, but when a woman does it, they are banished from society? Why did society shun the woman, even when she was the injured party?

She calmed Jim by promising to speak to Meghan when she visited her in the next couple of weeks. What she didn't tell him was that she had no intention of really interfering with Meghan's decision. She was going to St. Ives to have fun and perhaps meet her spirit animal again.

Chapter Thirty-Eight

Cornwall

Ana had never been to Cornwall and she was jumping with excitement at the thought of spending a week with Meghan and the group she had met at the festival. Did she need to call her Sky? While Jim was at work, she used a spare key to pack Meghan's clothes and other things she wanted from the house. Meghan's list was long and meticulous and included things such as "the big pot with the chipped lid, the warm coat in the back of the wardrobe, and the heavy gold bracelet," which was a present from a past lover. Unlike Ana, Meghan had always kept her own bank account as a little insurance. Over the years it had grown to several thousand pounds, and it would tie her over nicely until she decided what she was going to do with Jim. Clever Meghan. Not like Ana, who had been totally dependent on Bill.

Ana reached Cornwall late at night. She followed Google's directions until her path was blocked by a chain running across two boulders. There was no phone reception, so she parked her little convertible and walked up the hill until she reached the flickering lights ahead. In a flat meadow, she made out a circle of caravans and a roaring campfire in the middle. She heard singing and someone playing the guitar. A couple of battered sofas were arranged around the fire and she recognised Meghan curled up in one of them. She was in the arms of her new man and she looked beautiful.

The community was large and welcoming and totally relaxed. Ana felt at home right away, and that night she slept like a baby on a platform bed in one of the empty caravans. She saw the appeal of this life. As she drifted to sleep, she knew that Meghan would not be coming back any time soon.

In the morning, as she emerged from the caravan in search of coffee, the scenery took her breath away. In the dark she hadn't realised that the caravan was perched at the end of a cliff, with the little village of St. Ives nested underneath, turquoise beaches spreading on either side. She found the communal kitchen, made her coffee and brought it back to the swinging wicker chair suspended in front of her caravan. It was early and almost everyone was still asleep. She felt happy and it was the kind of happiness that sprung from deep inside her. She knew it was the real thing, pure and beautiful.

As it turned out, everyone in the community had a job, some less glamorous than others, but there were no slouches. Everyone worked and contributed, but what made it different was that they worked to live, not lived to work. For someone like Ana, who had been taught to fully dedicate herself to her work, this attitude was almost sacrilegious, but she could see the wisdom and the appeal of this approach. This was a happy place and Meghan had chosen well. Or perhaps she had been lucky.

Ana was meant to stay for a week, but the beauty and serenity of the place overtook her. For the first time in her life she felt like she had arrived, and that there was no reason for her to go anywhere else. Of course, there were plenty of reasons waiting for her in London, including her daughters and her job, but strangely she found that she didn't miss Hannah and Linda. To be precise, she didn't miss serving them, which was all that was required of her.

They had their friends and their lives, and with the egotism of the very young, they rarely spared a thought for their mother outside her role as caregiver. Society expected her to be fully dedicated to that role and to miss her children every second they were away, but Ana didn't feel that way. Should she feel guilty? Was she a bad mother? She brushed the thought away. The decisions she was going to make would be about her. Hannah and Linda were at the doorstep of life and everything lay ahead. She was past the halfway point, had narrowly escaped a serious illness, had a divorce under her belt, and her time to make it all worth it was finally here.

Ana, being the practical girl that she was, started planning the future. Could she realistically move to Cornwall? What would she do for a living? Linda had another two years of school. Was Bill able to take care of her? But, above all these practicalities, was this what she wanted? Would she still like living in a caravan when the weather changed and the wicked winds from the west battered the coast? It seemed ideal for a few days in the summer, but would these laid-back hippies annoy her over time? She was always a city girl, and this was life in the fringes of a small isolated village.

Even after a week, she started to miss Shoreditch and the ease of popping downstairs to Tesco Metro and Starbucks. Showering behind a curtain in a drafty shed was not ideal either. Meghan, in the throes of new love, was not bothered by any of this, but Ana's eyes were not clouded. And, of course, Ana was ambitious. She just didn't know what to be ambitious about.

With these thoughts in mind, after two weeks, she hugged her friend closely and reluctantly waved goodbye to this seductive hippy life on top of a cliff in Cornwall. She would visit again soon, but she wasn't going to stay.

A very big headache

It was clear to Ana and to those who knew her that she had changed. From the dissatisfied suburban housewife who bickered with her husband and yelled at her kids, she had been transformed into an island of calm. Even her ambitions had a serene quality about them. She wasn't anxious, fearful or worried. She didn't see the need to push for a solution. Even though she took her responsibilities seriously, the attention she gave them was proportional, and this made all the difference. Nothing could ruffle her, and her joy came from being content.

Many years ago, she saw a research study showing that happiness increases every year past the age of fifty. At the time, she dismissed the idea as preposterous. Growing old, sick and approaching death did not strike her a recipe for happiness. But now she understood. When you get to the wrong side of fifty, either by choice or by force, you evaluate where you are and often change direction. With the angst of youth gone and the need to climb the social ladder diminishing, you can free yourself to explore your true desires. What were hers? She wondered.

As a lifelong runner, Ana is a regular at her local park and she loves to run early in the morning when most of the world is still asleep. It's a form of meditation and she has always done some of her best thinking, gasping for breath around the large lake in the centre of the park. That particular morning, she was alone. In the early-morning light, she could see a light mist over the lake and hear the distant sound of the water birds. She ran by the park's café as the owner was arranging the chairs and getting ready to greet his first customers.

As she finished her second loop around the lake, Ana spotted a solitary figure at the café, sipping a coffee. A dog was patiently sitting next to the stranger. On the spur of the moment, she decided to share the stranger's solitude and have a coffee too. As she made her way to a nearby table, she stopped to pet the dog. As she bent down, she felt her legs turn to jelly. Her knees gave way and the world turned black.

When she came around, she saw the worried eyes of the café owner. The dog owner was speaking excitedly on the phone and she realised that he was calling an ambulance. Ana tried to sit up to indicate that she was alright—no ambulance was necessary—but a wave of nausea overtook her, and she lay back down.

She had a wicked headache, right in the middle of her forehead, probably from falling over, she assumed. The dog was looking down at her, wagging his tail. She tried to remember if there were two dogs, because that's what she was seeing. As she focused on one of the two, they slowly merged and became one. She tried to reach for her phone. Someone had to wake up the girls or they would be late for school. Her fingers didn't seem to be able to open the zipper. The café owner tried to help, but she couldn't make herself understood. The words were there, in her head, but they refused to form coherent sentences.

She closed her eyes, defeated. It was probably fallout from the excesses of the weekend in Cornwall. She worried that her sweaty clothes stunk, that the doctors would be able to tell that she had done ecstasy, that the girls would go to school without breakfast and that the stranger with the dog would be late for work. She was worried less by the fact that she couldn't speak or sit up.

At the hospital, she was rushed through A&E and an emergency MRI was arranged. It all seemed a bit over the top, as she was already feeling a lot better, but the doctor insisted that it was standard procedure, so she was swiftly admitted to the ward. Her sweaty clothes were exchanged for a hospital gown and she was quickly wheeled to the MRI room. Ana was given a pair of headphones that played an eclectic mix of hip hop. Perhaps hip hop is the best music to drown out the loud banging of the MRI machine.

Back at the ward, she messaged the girls and told them that she had a work emergency and that they should go to their dad's house for a few days. Then she called Sally to say that she wouldn't be coming to work for the next few days. Sally sounded like she was at the end of her tether with Ana's absences. Never mind. She wouldn't be staying long at the bank anyway. Ana was feeling absolutely fine and was totally unconcerned about the morning's adventure.

The next morning, two consultants came to her bedside and pulled the curtain closed. This was quite ridiculous as the curtain didn't block what they had to say. It did, however, hide her shocked face when she heard their verdict.

Her cancer had returned, and in a bad way, this time in her brain. There was a large tumour pressing against her optic nerve. There were other smaller ones scattered around her brain, making surgery useless. Absurdly, the thought that they were not able to saw through her skull brought her a moment of relief, before the doctor's next words plunged her into despair.

"Unfortunately, it is not curable," the younger of the two consultants announced, as he appeared to examine a speck on the floor.

She wanted to tell him that she was here on the bed in front of him, not on the floor. Someone should teach these guys some bedside manners. The older consultant was looking at her kindly.

"There are many things we can do to keep this tumour at bay and give you many asymptomatic months, maybe even a year." His voice trailed as he waited for her to say something. Was she meant to ask a question? She had questions, but she couldn't think of any. She looked at the consultant and opened and closed her mouth like a fish marooned on the beach. Finally, a question popped into her head.

"Will I lose my hair again?"

Chapter Forty

A friend in need, take two

She was discharged that afternoon, with instructions to return as soon as possible to discuss treatment. As soon as the doctors had left her bedside, she called Meghan and begged her to come back. Meghan, wonderful, amazing Meghan, had started packing while they were still on the phone and promised to be on a train to London that afternoon. Wearing her sweaty running clothes, Ana left the hospital, walking with care as if the tumour in her head might dislodge itself and start bouncing around if she made a sudden move.

The news was devastating, but it seemed unreal. She put one foot in front of the other as she walked on the Southbank. Runners were passing her left and right, and groups of tourists chatted away as they pointed and snapped pictures on their phones. Everybody was going about their business, but not her. She had a ticking bomb in her skull, and she was going to die. A wave of fear overtook her, and she started to run. Faster and faster she went until she was bumping into people going in the other direction. The buildings lost their definition as the tears streamed down her eyes. She couldn't outrun it. Everywhere she went the tumour would go with her. It was her lifelong companion.

At home she had a long shower. She could smell her sweat, an acrid unpleasant odour, unlike the *honest* sweat from running that she was used to. Ana realised she smelled of fear. Even though it was only approaching noon, she poured herself a large glass of wine and opened a large box of chocolates from Hotel Chocolat that she had been given at work for her birthday. She had resisted opening it knowing full well that once the seal was broken, they wouldn't last the week.

Meghan knocked on her door a few hours later. She found Ana swerving erratically and her first thought was that the tumour was making her do it. Then she spotted the empty wine bottle on the floor and the half-empty box of chocolates on the sofa and breathed a sigh of relief. Ana let out a wail and fell into Meghan's arms.

"I'm going to die," she informed Meghan. "Maybe soon. There will be no me, no Ana, nothing but a failed marriage and a mediocre and terribly short banking career." Meghan knew to keep quiet and let her vent her sadness and frustration. "It's so unfair! I was finally discovering what life was all about and now it will all end, and I'll lose my hair again!"

Meghan decided that the best strategy was to open another bottle of wine. The two friends talked well into the early hours of the morning. Actually, it was more like a monologue than a conversation. Meghan was a good listener. She didn't try to convince Ana that it was all going to be alright and Ana really appreciated that. She wasn't looking for advice, at least not yet.

The girls had to be told, appointments had to be made, and the practical side of a life cut short had to be dealt with. Meghan decided that the best thing she could do for her friend was make all these arrangements for her, and Ana was grateful.

They ended up telling the girls together. The news fell like rocks in a calm pond, and they cried and desperately hugged their mother until their sobs turned into hot tears. They all sat together on the sofa, even though it could only fit three. Their need for closeness was much greater than their need for comfort in that moment. Being squished together and feeling the warm resistance from Ana's body made them feel safe. Their breathing synchronised into one common inhale and exhale. They were breathing for each other, as if they were one body, one undivided entity.

They had questions, but Ana didn't have answers. The doctor mentioned a year, but what exactly did he say? A year to live? A year of treatment? A year before she had to go to the hospice? She hadn't heard anything else. A year, 365 days. As long as her gym membership. She thought about how quickly the temperature in the studio changed from warm to hot, and then to cold before becoming warm again. Not very long at all!

Hannah and Linda wanted to stay at home the next day, but Meghan bundled them into the train and send them off to school, despite their protestations. There was work to be done, and there would be plenty of time for tears once all hope had been extinguished. Ana, who had gone through cancer treatment already, knew exactly what was in store and was in no hurry to revisit the hospital. Meghan, who had only heard the diagnosis through the drunken ravings of her friend, had other ideas. She made an appointment for the very next day, and together they sat in the beige room waiting for the consultant to lay out the treatment options.

There weren't many. Ana's tumour will kill her in less than a year. She was grateful that her consultant was an honest man. He admitted that chemo wouldn't necessarily prolong her life, but it would certainly ruin the life that remained to her. Again, Ana found herself absurdly relieved that the best treatment for cancer was not going to treat her, and she could skip it without feeling FOMO. She was glad to have learned the meaning of FOMO—Fear Of Missing Out. It was the perfect word for this occasion.

FOMO makes cancer patients spend the last few months of their lives hairless and nauseous. When pressed, the doctor made it clear to her that she wouldn't have FOMO regarding the chemo. Radiotherapy would be used once the symptoms became severe, and he made it clear that she didn't need to worry at all about pain. This was the one thing he could guarantee. She would never be in pain. He couldn't tell them how long it would take for the symptoms to become severe and cripple her. It could take weeks or months. There was no way to tell.

The meeting was shorter than anticipated and they were sent away with nothing more than a prescription for severe headaches. Meghan felt uncomfortable about that and convinced Ana to get a second opinion. Ana didn't need much convincing. As soon as she left the doctor's office, she had second thoughts. Agreeing to not having any treatment felt like she had given up on life and agreed to be buried alive. Perhaps there was a way to fight it, and this doctor was too pessimistic. She wanted to fight it for the girls. They're too young to lose their mother.

The second opinion, courtesy of the excellent private insurance provided by the bank, presented a couple more options, including very risky surgery that would attempt to remove the large tumour. They could also do radiotherapy to try to shrink it, but it would severely affect her eyesight. Ana mentally put a tick next to "blind" on her list comprising "nauseous" and "hairless." She didn't like this doctor very much and there was a significant price attached to these treatments that may have contributed to his eagerness "to fight this." It's not a fight, she thought, and neither is it a capitulation to choose quality of life. She needed time to think it through, but not too much time. It was the one thing she didn't have, and shouldn't waste.

Chapter Forty-One

Ana's diary

What a wonderful life I've had! I only wish I'd realized it sooner.

— Colette

So, I am going to die. No more Ana. This body I worked so hard for will wither and rot. I will be forgotten. Not right away, but in a few years. Maybe in a decade I will be a faded memory, even to Hannah and Linda. They will forget my voice in just a year or so. I read about that. I'm thinking about recording things that they can listen to after I am gone. There are many diaries for them to read, but I need to go through them first and decide what I want my legacy to be. It's what they read in those diaries that will determine who I am after death.

I don't really care about my legacy outside my legacy to my daughters. I have always thought of legacies as something that only men worry about. I certainly don't. I never reached a conclusion as to the meaning of life, but I managed to reach a sort of nirvana, where I was happy with what I had and where I was in life. Perhaps this is the end goal for us humans. It certainly seems worthwhile.

Bill has been calling every day. He probably sees this latest diagnosis as his opportunity to redeem himself. He is the last person I want to see or talk to and thankfully Meghan has taken over informing him about practicalities. My biggest concern is for the girls. He will be the one to guide them through their first relationship, their university choices, their careers, and he is hopeless when it comes to choices. Bill doesn't make choices, choices make him. This is my most important job. Talking to the girls about choices. I must try to teach them what I have learned in the last few years. I am hopeful that they will remember, and even though they can't possibly understand at this young age, they eventually will.

It's hard to believe that I am dying. I feel extremely well. I go for runs every day, visit the gym, go shopping, all my normal activities. I don't go to work. This would have been really stupid. I got a super deal from the bank. Sally, terrified that she would have to deal with a puking, hairless employee once again, convinced her boss to give me six months paid leave. Sally doesn't know that I'm dying, and I'm not going to tell her yet. In fact, I'm only telling people on a need-to-know basis, and the number is small. Meghan, Bill, my family and the girls. No one else.

Speaking of mum and dad, they were distraught, and I feel bad for them. As a mother, I can't imagine anything worse than outliving my kids. They want to come and help but I don't need them yet, and thankfully the flat is too small for long-term guests. Meghan is undeterred by the nights on the sofa, but she misses her boyfriend. They see each other every other weekend, but I'm afraid I may outlive his dedication to her.

I have urged Meghan to get a short-term let and invite him to move in for the next few months. She is looking into it, but also likes the idea of moving in with her oldest daughter, who just got her first job. I insisted that this isn't ideal for her budding romance and her boyfriend will thank me for it. Regardless, she is pressing on with the divorce and I think that it's the right thing for her. Divorce settlements in this country have been generally fair to women and she should get a big one. Raising four kids and taking care of a perennial fifth one (Jim) is grounds for a generous pension. It took a while to convince her, but she now has a good lawyer and she's going for all she can get.

Tracy, my dear sister, is the only person who has been my past, knows my present, and would have been with me for the rest of my future. She is far away, and even though she's scheduled three trips to the UK to see me, they will be quick and tearful trips. She has a life to think of, and in America they don't give you time off to say year-long goodbyes. Tracy bought into the American dream: large mortgage, two car loans, and credit cards that are cracking from the weight of the debt she has piled on them. She needs her job and I understand that, but I would have liked to share with her some of what I have learned.

There is no time for anything. Last night I was rushed to St Thomas' Hospital after Linda came home from school to find me having a fit on the floor. I don't remember falling down, but there is a large cut on my forehead where I hit the corner of the coffee table. They're sending me back home this afternoon. There is nothing they can do, save the plaster on my forehead. I feel okay again, but I realise now that these symptoms will return with greater frequency.

My idea of a final road trip is out of the question. As much as the idea of going out in a giant fireball, or over a cliff like Thelma and Louise appeals to me, I don't want to risk taking other innocents with me on my last great journey. This leaves me to celebrate my life right here in Shoreditch and make the best of my symptom-free days. I always thought that I would want to spend my last few months in unusual luxury, but surprisingly, I don't really feel like putting together a bucket list of that sort.

My bucket list is quite different to the ones I've seen in the movies. I would like to go on another shamanic journey, and Meghan is looking into it as she is very keen as well. I would also like to create some lasting memories with Hannah and Linda to carry them through the difficult times that lie ahead. This is a critical year for Hannah. As much as I would like to take her and Linda on a trip—perhaps to Cornwall—I don't want to disrupt her schoolwork.

Christmas is a month away and more than likely it will be my last. We decided to make it big, so the whole family will be there. Even Tracy is coming over from America for the full two weeks that the kids are out of school. I am grateful, because this is her entire vacation for the whole year. I told her that I'd rather she came now that I am alive than make the trip for my funeral.

The presents have started piling up under our tree. I wonder what they have got me. It must be hard to buy presents for someone who only has a few months to live.

They assure me that I'll love my presents and of course I will.

I am afraid of dying. How can I not be? But I'm not as afraid as I was the first time around. I feel that a lot of what ailed me has been healed. When I faced death the first time around, I was restless and full of anger and regret. I am glad that I am not facing my demise consumed by those destructive feelings. My anger has been resolved. As for the regret, well that's a different story. When I started this diary, I felt like a failure. An interrupted career, a failed marriage, a life without a purpose. Now I realise that our purpose comes from inside, and our experiences are external and unrelated to that purpose. I have no regrets.

Here is my conclusion, which is simple and elegant: Our purpose is to resolve our constraints to becoming whole human beings, untainted by irrelevant and temporary upsets. Our goal should be to understand that conflict with other humans comes from their traumas, and we should forgive them for it. Even though my death will be untimely, I know that my purpose is complete. In Buddhism, enlightenment is when a Buddhist finds the truth about life and stops being reborn because he has reached Nirvana. This is exactly how I feel. My journey has landed me in Nirvana.

All my fear is physical, and I will have to come to terms with that. I just wish there was a light switch I could flick off instead of the medical saga I will have to endure. But there isn't, so I will endure what is to come with as much calmness as I can muster. My achievement in life was not what I thought I wanted, or even something that can be measured by conventional means. My totally ordinary life, as it will be judged by those around me, has really been quite extraordinary. I am awake!

The real meaning of enlightenment is to gaze with undimmed eyes on all darkness.

— Nikos Kazantzakis

Chapter Forty-Two

The end

Spiritual realization is to see clearly that what I perceive, experience, think, or feel is ultimately not who I am, that I cannot find myself in all those things that continually pass away.

— Eckhart Tolle

Ana passed away as the new year came over the horizon, surrounded by her family and her best friend Meghan. She really did love her Christmas presents, and felt fit and well right up to the end. On the morning of January 1st, 2019, the tumour in her brain brought on a massive brain aneurysm that killed her quickly and painlessly.

In her last moments, she felt wide awake, with her agenda successfully completed.

NOTE FROM THE AUTHOR

Word-of-mouth is crucial for any author to succeed. If you enjoyed this book, please leave a review online. Even if it's just a sentence or two. It would make all the difference and be very much appreciated.

Thanks!

Alexandra

www.loveisagame.net

.

ABOUT THE AUTHOR

Alexandra Filia is a successful entrepreneur, world traveler, and mother of two amazing daughters. As the founder and CEO of Powerchex, she set up a thriving pre-employment screening business in the UK, introducing novel ideas that led to the company winning multiple national awards.

An adventurer at heart, Alexandra sailed across the Atlantic and then lived on a boat in London with her baby daughters. Having sold the business, she now splits her time between Greece and the UK, writing books that help women on their quest for happiness.

The Woman Who Forgot Her Agenda is her fifth book.

www.loveisagame.net

BOOKS BY THE AUTHOR

Dream Series

Love Is A Game: A Marriage Proposal in 90 Days

The Good Breakup: Take a Deep Breath and Remember Who
You Really Are

Forever Young: An Anti-Ageing Guide for the Terrified

Novels

As If I Am Not There
(A novel about a young woman struggling with anorexia)

Printed in Great Britain
by Amazon

37553433R00142